NIGHT OF THE BOLD

(KINGS AND SORCERERS—BOOK 6)

MORGAN RICE

D1603598

For Kira Dean,
my hero, who has more courage than any knight.

CHAPTER ONE

Duncan walked through the ebbing flood, water splashing against his calves, flanked by dozens of his men as they trekked through the floating graveyard. Hundreds of Pandesian corpses floated by, bumping against his legs as he sloshed through what remained of the Everfall flood. As far as he could see stretched a sea of corpses, Pandesian soldiers washing up from the overflowing Canyon, being swept out to the desert in the receding waters. It was the solemn air of victory.

Duncan looked down at the Canyon, overflowing with water, still spewing out corpses by the minute as it bubbled over, and he turned and looked at the horizon, toward Everfall, where the gushing torrents had slowed to a trickle. Slowly, he felt the thrill of victory well up inside him. All around him, the air began to buzz with the victorious cheers of his stunned men, all trekking through the waters in disbelief, all slowly realizing that they had actually won. Against all odds, they had survived, had conquered the much greater legion. Leifall had come through, after all. Duncan felt a surge of gratitude to his loyal soldiers, to Leifall, Anvin, and most of all, his son. In the face of grim odds, none had backed down in fear.

There came a distant rumble, and Duncan checked the horizon and was overjoyed to see Leifall and his men of Leptus, Anvin and Aidan amongst them, White running at their feet, all returning from Everfall, riding back to reunite with them. They were joined by Leifall's small army, hundreds of men, their shouts of triumph audible even from here.

Duncan looked back to the north and spotted on the distant horizon a world filled with black. There, perhaps a day's ride away, sat the remainder of the Pandesian army, rallying, preparing to avenge their defeat. Next time they would not attack with ten thousand men, Duncan knew, but with a hundred thousand.

Duncan knew time was short. He had been lucky once, but there was no way he could withstand an attack from hundreds of thousands of soldiers, not even with every trick in the world. And he had exhausted all his tricks. He needed a new strategy, and he needed it fast.

As his men gathered around him, Duncan searched all the hard and earnest faces and knew these great warriors looked to him for leadership. He knew that whatever decision he made next would affect not just him but all of these great men—indeed, the entire fate of Escalon. He owed it to them all to choose wisely.

Duncan wracked his brain, willing the answer to come to him, pondering all the ramifications of any strategic move. All moves carried great risk, all carried dire repercussions, and all were even riskier than what he had done here in the canyon.

"Commander?" came a voice.

Duncan turned to see the serious face of Kavos, looking back at him with respect. Behind him, hundreds of men stared back, too. They were all awaiting direction. They had followed him to the brink and had come out alive, and they trusted him.

Duncan nodded, breathing deeply.

"We meet the Pandesians in the open field," he began, "and we lose. They outnumber us still a hundred to one. They are also better rested, armed and equipped. We would all be dead by sunfall."

Duncan sighed, his men hanging on his every word.

"Yet we cannot run," he continued, "nor should we. With the trolls, too, attacking, and the dragons circling, we have no time to hide, to fight a guerrilla war. Nor is hiding our way. We need a bold and quick and decisive strategy to defeat the invaders and rid our country of them once and for all."

Duncan fell silent for a long time, pondering the near impossible task ahead. All that could be heard was the sound of the wind rippling off the desert.

"What do you propose, Duncan?" Kavos finally prodded.

He looked back at Kavos, gripping and ungripping his halberd, staring back with intensity, as his words rang in his head. He owed these great warriors a strategy. A way not just to survive—but to victory.

Duncan pondered the terrain of Escalon. All battles, he knew, were won by terrain, and his knowing the terrain of his homeland was perhaps his one remaining advantage in this war. He reflected on all the places in Escalon where the terrain might offer a natural advantage. It would need to be a very special place indeed, a place where a few thousand men could fight off hundreds of thousands. There were few places in Escalon—few places anywhere—that could allow that.

Yet as Duncan recalled the legends and tales ingrained in him by his father and his father before him, as he recalled all the great battles he had studied from times of old, he found his mind turning to the battles that were most heroic, the most epic, the battles of few against many. Again and again, his mind returned to but one place: the Devil's Gulch.

The place of heroes. The place where few men had fought off an army, where all the great warriors of Escalon had been tested.

The Gulch offered the most narrow pass in all of Escalon, and it was perhaps the one place in the land where the terrain defined the battle. A wall of steep cliffs and mountains met the sea, leaving but a narrow corridor to pass through, forming the Gulch that had taken more than a few lives. It forced men to pass through single file. It forced armies to pass through single file. It created a bottleneck where a few warriors, if well placed and heroic enough, could fight off an entire army. At least, according to the legends.

"The Gulch," Duncan finally replied.

All eyes widened. Slowly, they nodded back in respect. The Gulch was a serious decision; it was a place of last resort. It was a place to go when there was no other place to go, a place for men to die or to live, for the land to be lost or to be saved. It was a place of legend. A place of heroes.

"The Gulch," Kavos said, nodding for a long time as he rubbed his beard. "Strong. Yet there remains one problem."

Duncan looked back.

"The Gulch is designed to keep invaders out—not in," he replied. "The Pandesians are already in. We could perhaps block it off and keep them in. But we want them out."

"Never once in our ancestors' time," Bramthos added, "has an invading army, once it crossed the Gulch, been forced to leave through it again. It is too late. They have already passed through it."

Duncan nodded back, thinking the same thoughts himself.

"I have considered this," he replied. "Yet there is always a way. Perhaps we can lure them back through it, to the other side. And then, once they are south, we can seal it off and make our stand."

The men stared back, clearly confused.

"And how do you propose we do that?" Kavos asked.

Duncan drew his sword, found a dry patch of sand, stepped forward, and began to draw. All the men huddled around close as his blade scratched the sand.

"A few of us will lure them through," he said, drawing a line in the sand. "The rest will wait on the other side, prepared to seal it. We shall make the Pandesians think they are pursuing us, that we are fleeing. My force, once it passes through, can circle back, through the tunnels, come back on this side of the Gulch, and seal it off. We can then all make a stand together."

Kavos shook his head.

"And what makes you think Ra will send his army through that gulch?"

Duncan felt determined.

"I understand Ra," he replied. "He craves our destruction. He craves complete and total victory. This will appeal to his hubris, and for that, he will send his entire army after us."

Kavos shook his head.

"The men that lure them through," he said, "will be exposed. It will be near impossible to make it back in time through the tunnels. Those men may likely be trapped and die."

Duncan nodded gravely.

"Which is why I shall lead those men myself," he said.

The man all looked back at him with respect. They stroked their beards, faces beset with concern and doubt, all clearly realizing how risky this was.

"Perhaps it could work," Kavos said. "Perhaps we can lure the Pandesian forces through and perhaps even seal them out. Yet even so, Ra won't send all his men. Stationed here are just his southern forces. He has other men, spread throughout our land. He has a mighty northern army, guarding the north. Even if we won this epic battle, we would not win the war. His men would still hold Escalon."

Duncan nodded back, thinking the same thoughts himself.

"This is why we shall split our forces," he replied. "Half of us will ride for the Gulch, while the other half will head north and attack Ra's northern army. Lead by you."

Kavos stared back at him with surprise.

"If we are to free Escalon, we must do it all at once," Duncan added. "You will lead the battle in the north. Lead them to your homeland, to Kos. Take the fight to the mountains. No one can fight there as well as you."

Kavos nodded, clearly liking the idea.

"And you, Duncan?" he asked in return, concern in his voice. "As poor as my odds are in the north, your odds in the Gulch are much worse."

Duncan nodded back and smiled. He clasped Kavos's shoulder.

"Better odds for glory, then," he replied.

Kavos smiled back with admiration.

"And what of the Pandesian fleet?" Seavig chimed in, stepping forward. "Even now they hold the port of Ur. Escalon cannot be free while they hold the seas."

Duncan nodded to his friend, laying a hand on his shoulder.

"Which is why you shall take your men and make for the coast," Duncan replied. "Use our hidden fleet and sail north, at night, up the Sorrow. Sail to Ur, and with cunning enough, perhaps you can defeat them."

Seavig stared back, rubbing his beard, his eyes alight with mischief and daring.

"You realize we will have a dozen ships against a thousand," he replied.

Duncan nodded back, and Seavig smiled.

"I knew there was a reason I liked you," Seavig replied.

Seavig mounted his horse, his men following, and he took off without another word, leading them all off into the desert, riding west for the sea

Kavos stepped forward, clasped Duncan's shoulder, and looked him in the eye.

"I always knew we would both die for Escalon," he said. "I only did not know we would die in such a glorious way. It shall be a death worthy of our ancestors. I thank you for that, Duncan. You have given us a great gift."

"And I you," Duncan replied.

Kavos turned, nodded to his men, and without another word, they all mounted their horses and took off, riding north, for Kos. They all rode off with eager shouts, raising up a great cloud of dust as they went.

That left Duncan standing there alone with several hundred men, all looking to him for direction. He turned and faced them.

"Leifall approaches," he said, watching them near on the horizon. "When they arrive, we shall all ride for the Gulch as one."

Duncan went to mount his horse, when suddenly, a voice cut through the air:

"Commander!"

Duncan turned in the opposite direction, and he was shocked at what he saw. There, from the east, a lone figure was approaching, walking toward them through the desert. Duncan's heart pounded as he watched her. It could not be possible.

His men parted ways on all sides as she approached. Duncan's heart skipped a beat, and he slowly felt his eyes filling with tears of joy. He could hardly believe it. There, approaching him, like an apparition from the desert, was his daughter.

Kyra.

Kyra walked toward them, alone, a smile on her face, heading right for him. Duncan was baffled. How had she arrived here? What was she doing here? Why was she alone? Had she walked all this way? Where was Andor? Where was her dragon?

None of it made any sense.

And yet there she was, in the flesh and blood, his daughter returned to him. Seeing her made him feel as if his soul was being restored. All felt right in the world, even if just for a moment.

"Kyra," he said, stepping forward eagerly.

The soldiers parted ways as Duncan walked forward, smiling, holding out his arms, eager to embrace her. She smiled too, throwing her arms out as she walked toward him. It made his entire life worthwhile just to know that she was alive.

Duncan took the final steps, so excited to embrace her, and as she stepped forward and embraced him, he wrapped his arms around her.

"Kyra," he gushed, tearing. "You're alive. You've returned to me."

He could feel the tears streaming down his face, tears of joy and relief.

Yet strangely, as he held her, she was still, silent in return.

Slowly, Duncan began to realize that something was wrong. A split second before he realized, his world was suddenly filled with blinding pain.

Duncan gasped, unable to catch his breath. His tears of joy quickly morphed to tears of pain, as he found himself breathless. He couldn't process what was happening; instead of a loving embrace, he felt a cold shaft of steel puncturing his ribs, being driven all the way inside. He felt a hot sensation gushing down his stomach, felt himself numb, unable to breathe, to think. The pain was so blinding, so searing, so unexpected. He looked down and saw a dagger in his heart, and he stood there in shock.

He looked up at Kyra, looked into her eyes, and as horrific as the pain was, the pain of her betrayal was worse. Dying did not bother him. But dying by his daughter's hand tore him to pieces.

As he felt the world begin to spin beneath him, Duncan blinked, baffled, trying to understand why the person he loved most in the world would betray him.

Yet Kyra only smiled back, showing no remorse.

"Hello, Father," she said. "So nice to see you again."

CHAPTER TWO

Alec stood in the dragon's mouth, gripping the Unfinished Sword with trembling hands, dazed, as the dragon's blood gushed down on him like a waterfall. He looked out from between the rows of razor-sharp teeth, each as large as he, and braced himself as the dragon plummeted straight down for the ocean below. He felt his stomach dropping through his throat as the icy waters of the Bay of Death rushed up to greet him. He knew that if he was not killed by the impact, he would be crushed by the dead dragon's weight.

Alec, still in shock that he'd managed to kill this great beast, knew that the dragon, with all its weight and speed, would sink to the bottom of the Bay of Death, and would take him with it. The Unfinished Sword could slay a dragon—but no sword could stop his descent. Worse, the dragon's jaws, now lax, were closing in on him as its jaw muscles relaxed, clamping down to become a cage from which Alec could never escape. He knew he had to move fast if he had any chance of survival.

As the blood gushed down onto his head from the roof of the dragon's mouth, Alec extracted the sword and, as the jaws nearly closed, braced himself and leapt. He shrieked as he fell through the icy air, the dragon's razor-sharp teeth scraping his back, slicing his flesh, and for a moment, his shirt snagged on the dragon's tooth, and he did not think he would make it. Behind him he heard the great jaws clamp shut, felt his shirt rip, a piece torn off—and finally, he was in free-fall.

Alec flailed as he dropped through the air, bracing himself for the black, swirling waters below.

Suddenly there came a splash, and Alec was in shock as he plunged into the frigid waters, the icy temperature taking his breath away. The last thing he saw as he looked up was the dragon's dead body, plunging down near him, about to impact the bay.

The dragon's body hit the surface with an awful crash, sending huge waves of water up in either direction. Luckily, it just missed Alec, and the wave instead crested out and away from its corpse. It carried Alec high up a good twenty feet away before it stopped—and then, to Alec's dread, it began to suck down everything around it in a giant whirlpool.

Alec swam with all his might to get away, yet he could not. Try as he did, the next thing he knew, he was being sucked down in the vast whirlpool, beneath the depths.

Alec swam as best he could while still clutching the sword, already a good twenty feet below the surface, kicking and plunging in the freezing waters. He kicked for the surface, desperate, sunlight sparkling high above, and as he did, he saw massive sharks begin to swim toward him. He just spotted the hull of the ship bobbing in the waters high above and he knew he had but moments to make it if he were to survive.

With one last kick Alec finally surfaced, gasping for air; a moment later, he felt strong hands grabbing at him. He looked up to see Sovos yanking him on board the ship, and a second later he was up in the air, still grasping the sword.

Yet he sensed motion out of the corner of his eye and turned to see a massive red shark leaping out of the water, aiming for his leg. There was no time.

Alec felt the sword humming in his hand, telling him what to do. It was like no other feeling he'd ever felt. He swung and shrieked as he brought it down with all his might, using both hands.

There followed the sound of steel cutting through flesh, and Alec watched with shock as the Unfinished Sword hacked the huge shark in half. The red waters quickly teemed with sharks, eating the pieces.

Another shark leapt up for his feet, yet this time Alec felt himself yanked high up and he landed on the deck with a thud.

He rolled and groaned, covered in aches and bruises, and breathed hard with relief, spent, dripping wet. Someone immediately covered him in a blanket.

"As if killing a dragon weren't enough," Sovos said with a smile, standing over him, handing him a flask of wine. Alec took a long swig, and it warmed his stomach.

The ship was teeming with soldiers, all in an excited, chaotic state. Alec was not surprised: it was not often, after all, that a dragon was felled by a sword. He looked over and saw on the deck, amidst the crowd, Merk and Lorna, clearly rescued from bobbing in the waters before. Merk looked to him like a rogue, possibly an assassin, while Lorna was stunning, with an ethereal quality. They were both dripping wet and looked dazed, and happy to be alive.

Alec noticed all the soldiers staring back at him, awestruck, and he slowly rose to his feet, in shock as he realized himself what he had just achieved. They looked from the sword, dripping wet in his hand, up to him, as if he were a god. He could not help but look down at the sword himself, feeling the weight of it in his hand, like a living thing. He stared down at the mysterious, gleaming metal as if it were a foreign object and he relived in his mind the moment he had stabbed the dragon, his shock at its puncturing its flesh. He marveled at the power of this weapon.

Perhaps even more than that, Alec could not help but wonder who *he* was. How was he, a simply boy from a simple village, able to slay a dragon? What did destiny have in store for him? He was beginning to feel it would be no ordinary destiny.

Alec heard the snapping of a thousand jaws, and he looked over the rail to see a school of red sharks now feasting on the dragon's huge carcass, floating at the surface. The black waters of the Bay of Death were now blood-red. Alec watched the floating carcass, and it sank in that he had really done it. Somehow, he had killed a dragon. He, alone, in all of Escalon.

Great shrieks filled the sky, and Alec looked up to see dozens more dragons circling in the distance, breathing great columns of flame, eager for vengeance. While they all stared own at him, some seemed afraid to approach. Several flew off from the pack as they spotted their fellow dragon floating dead in the water.

Others, though, screeched in fury and dove right for him.

As he watched them plummet, Alec did not wait. He ran for the stern, jumped onto the rail, and faced them. He felt the power of the sword coursing through him, egging him on, and as he stood there, he felt a new steely determination. He felt as if the sword were driving him. He and the weapon were now one.

The pack of dragons descended right for him. A huge one with glowing green eyes led them, shrieking as it breathed down flame. Alec held the sword high, feeling the vibration in his hand, lending him courage. The very fate of Escalon, he knew, was at stake.

Alec felt a surge of courage he'd never known as he let out a battle cry himself; as he did, the sword became aglow. An intense burst of light shot forth, rising up, stopping the wall of flame halfway in the sky. It continued on until it made the flame reverse course, and as Alec slashed the sword again, the dragon shrieked as its own column of flame encapsulated it. In a great ball of fire, the dragon shrieked and flailed as it fell straight down and plunged into the waters.

Another dragon dove down, and again Alec raised the sword, stopping the wall of flame, killing it. Another dragon came in low, and as it did, it lowered its talons, as if to scoop Alec up. Alec turned and slashed and was shocked as the sword chopped off its legs. The dragon screeched, and in the same motion Alec swung again, slashing its side, opening a huge gash. The dragon crashed into the ocean, and as it flapped there, unable to fly, it was set upon by a mass of sharks.

Another dragon, a small red one, swooped down low from the other side, its jaws wide open—and as it did, this time Alec allowed his instincts to lead him and leapt up into the air. The sword lent him power, and he leapt higher than he could imagine, over the dragon's head, and landed on its back.

The dragon shrieked and bucked, but Alec held on tight. It could not cast him off.

Alec felt himself stronger than the dragon, able to command it.

"Dragon!" he called out. "I command you! Attack!"

The dragon had no choice but to turn and fly up, right into the flock of descending dragons, a dozen of them still coming down. Alec faced them fearlessly, flying up to meet them, holding the sword before him. As they met in the sky, Alec slashed the sword again and again, with a power and speed he did not know he possessed. He sliced off one dragon's wing, then sliced another's throat, then stabbed another in the side of the neck, then spun and cut off another's tail. One at a time the dragons plummeted down through the sky, crashing into the waters, causing a whirlpool in the bay below.

Alec did not relent. He attacked the flock again and again, criss-crossing the skies, never retreating. Caught up in the whirlwind, he barely noticed when finally the few remaining dragons turned, screeched, and flew off, afraid.

Alec could hardly believe it. Dragons. *Afraid.*

Alec looked below. He saw how high he was, saw the Bay of Death laid out below, saw hundreds of ships, most aflame, and thousands of trolls floating, dead. The Isle of Knossos, too, was aflame, its great fort in ruins. It was a sprawling scene of chaos and destruction.

Alec spotted his fleet and directed the dragon lower. When they neared, Alec raised the sword and plunged it into the dragon's back. It screeched and began to plummet, and as they neared the water, Alec leapt and landed in the waters beside the ship.

Immediately, ropes were thrown, and Alec was hoisted back inside.

As he landed back on the deck, this time, he did not shiver. He no longer felt cold, or tired, or weak, or afraid. He felt, instead, a power he never knew. He felt filled with courage, with strength. He felt himself being reborn.

He had killed a flock of dragons.

And nothing in Escalon could stop him now.

CHAPTER THREE

Vesuvius, awakened by the feeling of sharp claws crawling on the back of his hand, peeled open one eye, the other still sealed shut. He looked up, disoriented, to find himself lying face first in the sand, ocean waves crashing behind him, icy water rushing up the back of his legs. He remembered. After that epic battle he had washed up on the shores of the Bay of Death; he wondered how long he had lay here, unconscious. The tide was now slowly creeping in, preparing to carry him away if he had not awakened. Yet it was not the cold of the waters that woke him—it was the creature on his hand.

Vesuvius looked over at his hand, stretched out on the sand, and saw a large purple crab digging a claw into his hand, tearing out a small piece of his flesh. It took its time, as if Vesuvius were a corpse. With each dig, Vesuvius felt a shock wave of pain.

Vesuvius could not blame the creature; he looked out and saw thousands of corpses sprawled all over this beach, the remnants of his troll army. They all lay there, covered by the purple crabs, the click-clack of their claws filling the air. The stink of decaying trolls overwhelmed him, made him nearly gag. This crab on his hand was clearly the first that had dared venture all the way to Vesuvius. The others likely sensed he was still alive and bided their time. Yet this one brave crab had taken his chances. Dozens more were turning his way now, tentatively following his lead. In moments, Vesuvius knew, he would be covered, eaten alive by this small army—if he wasn't first sucked out to sea by the freezing tides of the Bay of Death.

Feeling a hot flash of rage, Vesuvius reached over with his free hand, grabbed the purple crab, and slowly squeezed. The crab tried to get away—but Vesuvius would not allow it to. It flailed wildly, trying to reach Vesuvius with its pinchers, but he held tight, preventing it from spinning around. He squeezed harder and harder, slowly, taking his time, taking great pleasure in inflicting pain. The creature screeched, hissing an awful high-pitched noise, as Vesuvius slowly squeezed his hand into a fist.

Finally, it exploded. Gobs of purple blood dripped onto his hand, as Vesuvius heard the satisfying crack of the shell. He dropped it, smashed to a pulp.

Vesuvius pulled himself up to one knee, still wobbly, and as he did, dozens of crabs scurried away, clearly shocked to see the dead rise. A chain reaction began, and as he stood, thousands of crabs scattered, leaving the beach empty as Vesuvius took his first steps on shore. He walked through the graveyard and slowly, it all came flooding back.

The battle of Knossos. He had been winning, about to destroy Lorna and Merk, when those dragons had arrived. He recalled falling from the island; losing his army; recalled his fleet aflame; and finally, nearly drowning himself. It had been a rout, and he burned with shame at the thought of it. He turned and looked back out at the bay, the place of his defeat, and saw, in the distance, the Isle of Knossos still aflame. He saw the remnants of his fleet, floating, smashed into pieces, some partial ships still aflame. And then he heard a shriek high above. He looked up and blinked.

Vesuvius could not conceive what he saw before him. It could not be. Dragons were falling from the sky, plummeting into the bay, unmoving.

Dead.

High above, he saw a lone man riding one, battling them all as he clung to the back of a dragon, wielding a sword. Finally, the rest of the flock turned and fled.

He looked back to the waters and saw, on the horizon, dozens of ships, flying the banners of the Lost Isles, and he watched as the man dropped from the last dragon and returned to the ships. He spotted the girl, Lorna, the assassin, Merk, and it burned him to know they had survived.

Vesuvius looked back to the shore and as he examined his troll nation dead, eaten by crabs or taken by the tide and eaten by sharks, he had never felt so alone. He was, he realized with shock, the sole survivor of the army he had brought.

Vesuvius turned and looked north, at the mainland of Escalon, and he knew that somewhere, far north, the Flames had been lowered. Right now, his people were leaving Marda, raiding Escalon, millions of trolls migrating south. After all, Vesuvius had succeeded in reaching the Tower of Kos, in destroying the Sword of Flames, and surely by now his nation had crossed over and was tearing Escalon to bits. They needed leadership. They needed him.

Vesuvius may have lost this battle—but, he had to remember, he had won the war. His greatest moment of glory, the moment he'd awaited his entire life, was still awaiting him. The time had come for him to claim the mantle, to lead his people to complete and total victory.

Yes, he thought, as he stood straighter, brushing off the pain, the wounds, the freezing cold. He had gotten what he had come for. Let the girl and her people flail about on the ocean. After all, he had the destruction of Escalon before him. He could always return and kill her later. He smiled at the thought. He would kill her indeed. He would tear her limb to limb.

Vesuvius took off at a jog, then, soon, a full-fledged run. He would head north. He would meet his nation. And he would lead them on the greatest battle of all time.

It was time to destroy Escalon for now and forever.

Soon, Escalon and Marda would be one.

CHAPTER FOUR

Kyle watched in awe as the fissure in the earth widened, thousands of trolls falling to their deaths, flailing, deep into the bowels of the earth. Alva stood close by, staff raised, and intense rays of light shone down from it, so bright that Kyle had to shield his eyes. He was obliterating the army of trolls, single-handedly protecting the north. Kyle had fought with all he had, as had Kolva beside him, and while they had taken out dozens of trolls in fierce hand-to-hand combat before falling wounded, their resources were limited. Alva was the only thing stopping the trolls from overrunning Escalon.

The trolls soon realized the fissure was killing them, and they stopped on the far side, fifty feet away, realizing they could no longer advance. They looked out at Alva and Kolva and Kyle and Dierdre and Marco, eyes filled with frustration. As the fissure continued to spread their way, they turned, and panic in their eyes, they fled.

Soon the great rumbling thundered away, and all fell silent. The tide of trolls had stopped. Were they fleeing back to Marda? Regrouping to invade elsewhere? Kyle could not be sure.

As everything quieted, Kyle lay there, in agony from his wounds. He watched as Alva slowly lowered his staff and the light dimmed around him. Alva then turned to him, held out a palm, and laid it on Kyle's forehead. Kyle felt a rush of light enter his body, felt himself warming, lightening, and within moments, he felt himself completely healed. He sat up, in shock, feeling himself again—and overflowing with gratitude.

Alva knelt at Kolva's side, laid his hand on his stomach, and healed him, too. Within moments Kolva stood, clearly surprised to be back on his feet, light glowing from his eyes. Dierdre and Marco were next, and as Alva laid his palms on them, they, too were healed. He reached out with his staff and touched Leo and Andor, too, and they rose to their feet, all of them healed by Alva's magical power before their wounds finished them off for good.

Kyle stood there, amazed, witnessing firsthand the power of this magical being he had only heard rumors of for most of his life. He knew he was in the presence of a true master. He also sensed that it was a presence that was fleeting; a master that could not stay.

"You have done it," Kyle said, filled with awe and gratitude. "You have stopped the entire nation of trolls."

Alva shook his head.

"I have not," he replied deliberately, his voice measured, ancient. "I have only slowed them. A great and terrible destruction still comes our way."

"Yet how?" Kyle pressed. "The fissure—they could never cross it. You've killed so many thousands of them. Are we not safe?"

Alva shook his head sadly.

"You have not even begun to see the tip of this nation. Millions more have yet to advance. The great battle has begun. The battle that will decide the fate of Escalon."

Alva walked through the rubble of the Tower of Ur, picking his way with his staff, and Kyle studied him, puzzled as always by this enigma. He finally turned to Dierdre and Marco.

"You crave to return to Ur, do you not?" he asked them.

Dierdre and Marco nodded back, hope in their eyes.

"Go," he commanded.

They stared back, clearly baffled.

"But there is nothing left there," she said. "The city was destroyed. Flooded. The Pandesians rule it now."

"To return there would be to return to our deaths," Marco chimed in.

"For now," Alva replied. "But you will be needed there soon, when the great battle comes."

Dierdre and Marco, needing no prodding, turned, mounted Andor together, and galloped away, south into the woods, back toward the city of Ur.

Leo remained back, by Kyle's side, and Kyle stroked his head.

"You think of me and you think of Kyra, don't you boy?" Kyle asked Leo.

Leo whined back affectionately, and Kyle could tell he would stay by his side and protect him as if he were Kyra. He sensed a great fighting partner in him.

Kyle looked back, questioning, as Alva turned and stared at the woods to the north.

"And us, my master?" Kyle asked. "Where are we needed?"

"Right here," Alva said.

Kyle stared at the horizon, joining him in looking north toward Marda.

"They are coming," Alva added. "And we three are the last and final hope."

CHAPTER FIVE

Kyra was flooded with panic as she struggled in the spider's web, writhing, desperate to get free as the massive creature crawled for her. She did not want to look, but could not help it. She turned and was filled with dread to see a hissing, massive spider, creeping down at her, one huge leg at a time. It stared back with its huge red eyes, raised its long, fuzzy black legs, and opened its mouth wide, revealing yellow fangs, saliva dripping from them. Kyra knew she had but moments to live—and that this would be an awful way to die.

As she writhed, Kyra heard the clatter all around her of bones in the web; she looked and saw the remains of all the victims who had died here before her, and she knew her chances of survival were slim. She was stuck to the web, and there was nothing she could do.

Kyra closed her eyes, knowing she had no other choice. She could not rely on the external world. She had to look within. She knew the answer did not lie in her external strength, in her external weaponry. If she relied on the external world, she would die.

Internally, though, her power, she sensed, was vast, infinite. She had to tap her inner strength, had to summon the powers she feared to face. She had to finally understand what drove her, understand the sum result of all her spiritual training.

Energy. That was what Alva taught her. *When we rely on ourselves, we use but a fraction of our energy, a fraction of our potential. Tap into the world's energy. The entire collective universe is waiting to assist you.*

It was coursing through her veins, she felt it. It was that special something she had been born with, that her mother had passed down to her. It was the power that coursed through everything, like a river flowing beneath the earth. It was the same power she had always had a hard time trusting in. It was the deepest part of herself, and the part she still did not completely trust. It was the part that she feared the most, more so than any enemy. She wanted to summon her mother, desperate for her help. Yet she knew she could not reach her here, in this land of Marda. She was entirely on her own. Perhaps this, being utterly alone, dependent on no one else, was the final leg of her training.

Kyra closed her eyes, knowing it was now or never. She sensed she had to become bigger than herself, bigger than this world she saw before her. She forced herself to focus on the energy within, and then, the energy all around her.

Slowly, Kyra tuned in. She sensed the energy of the web, of the spider; she could feel it coursing through her. She slowly allowed it to become a part of her. She no longer struggled against it. She allowed herself, instead, to become one with it.

Kyra felt herself slow down; she felt time slow down. She tuned in on the smallest detail, heard everything, felt everything around her.

Suddenly, Kyra felt a flash of energy, and she knew, for the first time, that all of the universe was one. She felt all the walls of separation come down, felt the barrier dissolve between the external and internal worlds. She felt that the distinction itself was false.

As she did, she felt a rush of energy, as if a dam had released inside her. Her palms burned as if they were on fire.

Kyra opened her eyes and saw the spider, so close now, looking down at her, preparing to pounce. She turned and saw her staff, feet away, stuck in the web. She reached out, no longer doubting herself. She summoned the staff, and as she did, it sailed through the air, right into her waiting palm. She clutched it tight.

Kyra used her power, knowing she was stronger than all she saw before her, and trusted herself. As she did, she raised her arm holding the staff, and it snapped free of the web.

She wheeled, and just as the spider closed its fangs for her, she reached over and jabbed her staff inside its mouth.

The spider let out a horrible screeching noise, and Kyra pried the staff deep into its mouth, turning it sideways. It tried to close its jaws, but it could not, the staff prying its mouth open.

But then, to Kyra's shock, it suddenly closed its jaws and snapped the ancient staff into pieces. It broke that which could not be broken, shattering it in its mouth like a toothpick. This beast was more powerful than she had imagined.

The spider pounced for her, and as it did, time slowed. Kyra felt everything snap into focus. She felt, deep down, that she could free herself, that she could be faster than it was.

Kyra snapped forward, freeing herself, and rolled in the web; when its fangs lowered, they tore open the web instead of her.

As Kyra focused, she felt, for the first time, a faint buzz in the air, felt something summoning her. She turned and stared at what, on the far side of the web, was what she had journeyed to Marda for: the Staff of Truth. There it sat, lodged in a block of black granite, ethereal, glowing under the midnight sky.

Kyra felt an intense connection with it, felt her palms tingling as she reached out with her right hand. She let out the greatest battle cry of her life, and she knew, she just knew, that the staff would obey her.

Suddenly, Kyra felt the earth shake beneath her. She knew she was drawing the weapon out from the very core of the earth, and for a glorious moment, she no longer doubted herself, her powers, or the universe.

A great noise followed, that of stone grating against stone, and Kyra watched with awe as the staff slowly rose, released from the granite. It lifted slowly, then flew through the air, its black, jeweled shaft landing in Kyra's right palm. She grasped it and she felt alive. It was like grasping a snake, like holding onto a living thing.

Without hesitating, Kyra spun and brought it down, just as the spider came for her. The staff suddenly morphed into a blade, and it sliced the massive web in half.

The spider, screeching, fell to the ground, clearly stunned.

Kyra spun around and sliced the web again, freeing herself completely and landing on her feet. She held the staff with both hands high above her head, just as the beast lunged for her. She faced it bravely, stepping forward and slashing at it with the Staff of Truth with all her might. She felt the staff cut through the spider's thick body. It let out an awful screech, as she sliced the spider in half.

Thick, black blood gushed from it, as the spider fell to her feet, dead.

Kyra stood there holding the staff, arms trembling, feeling a rush of energy unlike anything she had ever felt. She felt that she had changed in that moment. She felt she had become more powerful, that she would never be the same again. She felt all the doors had opened, and that anything was possible.

High above, the skies thundered, and lightning cracked. Scarlet lightning shot across the clouds, layering it with streaks, as if the clouds were running with lava. There followed a tremendous roar, and Kyra was overjoyed to see Theon bursting through the clouds. The barrier, she sensed, had been lowered as she drew the staff. For the first time, she knew that she was the one destined to change everything.

Theon landed at her feet, and without pausing, she mounted his back and they rose high into the air. Thunder rumbled all around them as they flew through the skies, heading south, away from Marda, toward Escalon. Kyra knew she had descended to the deepest levels and had prevailed, that she had passed her final test.

And now, the Staff of Truth in hand, she had a war to wage.

CHAPTER SIX

As she sailed away, Lorna watched the still-burning isle of Knossos fade into the horizon, and her heart broke inside her. She stood at the bow of the ship, gripping the rail, Merk at her side and the fleet of the Lost Isles behind her, and could feel all the eyes upon her. This beloved isle, home to the Watchers, to the brave warriors of Knossos, was no more. Up in flames, its glorious fort destroyed, the beloved warriors who had stood guard for thousands of years were now all dead, killed by the wave of trolls, and finished off by the flock of dragons.

Lorna sensed motion and turned to see, stepping up beside her, Alec, the boy who had killed the dragons, who had finally made the Bay of Death fall silent. He stood there, looking as dazed as she, holding his sword, and she felt a wave of gratitude toward him, and toward that weapon he held his hands. She glanced down at it, the Unfinished Sword, a thing of beauty, and could feel the intense energy coming off of it. She recalled the dragons' death, and she knew that in his hands he held the fate of Escalon.

Lorna was grateful to be alive. She knew that she and Merk would have met a fateful end in the Bay of Death had these men of the Lost Isles not arrived. Yet she also felt a wave of guilt for those who had not survived. What pained her most was that she had not foreseen this. Her entire life, she had foreseen everything, all the twists and turns of fate in her lonely life standing guard in the Tower of Kos. She had foreseen the trolls' arrival, had foreseen Merk's arrival, and had even foreseen the Sword of Flames being destroyed. She had foreseen the great battle at the Isle of Knossos— yet she had not foreseen its outcome. She had not foreseen the isle in flames, had not foreseen these dragons. She was doubting her own powers, and that stung her more than anything.

How could this happen? she wondered. The only answer could be that the destiny of Escalon was changing moment to moment. What had been written for thousands of years was being unwritten. The fate of Escalon, she sensed, hung in the balance, and was now amorphous.

Lorna sensed all the eyes of the ship on her, all wanting to know where to go next, what fate held in store for them as they sailed from the burning isle. With the world burning in chaos, they all looked to her for the answer.

As Lorna stood there, she closed her eyes, and slowly, she could feel the answer welling up inside her, telling her where they were needed most. Something was obscuring her vision, though. With a start, she remembered. Thurn.

Lorna opened her eyes and searched the waters below, watching every floating body that passed by, the sea of corpses bumping against the hull. The other sailors, too, had been searching for hours, scanning the faces with her, and yet they had not been successful.

"My lady, the ship awaits your command," Merk prodded gently.

"We have searched the waters for hours," Sovos added. "Thurn is dead. We must let him go."

Lorna shook her head.

"I sense he is not," she countered.

"I, more than anyone, wish that were so," Merk replied. "I owe him my life. He saved us from the dragons' breath. Yet we saw him catch fire and plummet to the sea."

"Yet we did not see him die," she replied.

Sovos sighed.

"Even if he somehow survived the fall, my lady," Sovos added, "he could not have survived these waters. We must let him go. Our fleet needs direction."

"No," she said, decisive, her voice ringing with authority. She could feel it rising within her, a premonition, a tingling between her eyes. It was telling her that Thurn was alive down there, somewhere amidst the wreckage, amidst the thousands of floating bodies.

Lorna scanned the waters, waiting, hoping, listening. She owed him that much, and she never turned a back on a friend. The Bay of Death was eerily quiet, with all the trolls dead, the dragons gone; and yet still it carried a sound of its own, the non-stop howling of the wind, the splashing of a thousand whitecaps, the groaning of their ship as it was rocked nonstop. As she listened, the gales of wind grew more fierce.

"A storm brews, my lady," Sovos finally said. "We must sail. We need direction."

She knew they were right. And yet, she could not let go.

Just as Sovos opened his mouth to speak, suddenly Lorna felt a rush of excitement. She leaned over and spied something in the distance, bobbing in the waters, carried by the currents toward the ship. She felt a tingling in her gut, and she knew it was him.

"THERE!" she cried.

The men rushed to the railing and stared over the edge, and they all saw it, too: there was Thurn, floating in the water. Lorna wasted no time. She took two big steps, jumped off the rail, and dove, head first, falling twenty feet through the air down for the icy waters of the bay.

"Lorna!" Merk cried out behind her, concern in his voice.

Lorna saw the red sharks swarming below, and understood his concern. They were circling Thurn, but while they prodded him, she saw they hadn't yet been able to pierce his armor. Thurn was lucky, she realized, to still be in his armor, the only thing saving his life— and luckier still that he was grasping a plank of wood, keeping him afloat. Yet the sharks were now swarming in greater force, becoming more bold, and she knew his time was limited.

She also knew the sharks would come for her, and yet she would not hesitate, not when his life was in danger. She owed him that much.

Lorna landed in the water, in shock at the icy cold, and without pausing, kicked and swam beneath the surface until she reached him, using her power to swim faster than the sharks. She put her arms around him, grabbing him, sensing he was alive, though unconscious. The sharks began to swim for her, and she braced herself, prepared to do whatever she had to do to keep them alive.

Lorna suddenly saw ropes landing around her, and she grabbed on tight and felt herself yanked backwards quickly, flying through the air. It was not a moment too soon: a red shark leapt from the water and snapped for her legs, just missing.

Lorna, holding Thurn, was yanked through the air, rising in the freezing wind, swaying wildly as they smashed against the hull of the ship. A moment later they were pulled up by the crew, and before she went back on board, she caught a last glimpse of the sharks swarming below, furious at having lost their meal.

Lorna landed on the deck with a thud, Thurn in her arms, and as they did, she immediately turned him over and examined him. Half of his face was disfigured, burnt by the flames, yet he had, at least, survived. His eyes were closed. At least they were not open to the sky; that was a good sign. She put her hands on his heart, and she felt something. However faint, there was a heartbeat.

Lorna rested her palms on his heart, and as she did, she felt a rush of energy, an intense heat pouring through her palms and into him. She summoned her powers and willed for Thurn to come back to life.

Thurn suddenly opened his eyes and sat upright with a gasp, breathing heavily, spitting out water. He coughed and the other men rushed forward and wrapped him in furs, warming him. Lorna was elated. She watched the color return to his face, and she knew he would live.

Lorna suddenly felt a warm fur being draped over her shoulder, and she turned to see Merk standing over her, smiling down, helping her to her feet.

The men soon crowded around her, looking at her with even more respect.

"And now?" he asked earnestly, coming up beside her. He nearly had to shout to be heard over the wind, the groaning of their rocking ship.

Lorna knew their time was scarce. She closed her eyes and reached her palms up to the sky, and slowly, she felt the fabric of the universe. With the Sword of Flames destroyed, Knossos gone, the dragons fled, she needed to know where Escalon needed them most in its time of crisis.

She suddenly felt the vibration of the Unfinished Sword beside her, and she knew. She turned and looked at Alec, and he stared back, clearly waiting.

She felt his special destiny rising up within her.

"You shall pursue the dragons no more," she said. "Those that fled will not come to you—they fear you now. And if you seek them out, you will not find them. They have gone to battle elsewhere in Escalon. The mission to destroy them is now someone else's."

"Then what, my lady?" he asked, clearly surprised.

She closed her eyes and sensed the answer coming to her.

"The Flames," Lorna replied, feeling the answer with certainty. "They must be restored. It is the only way to keep Marda from destroying Escalon. That is what matters most now."

Alec seemed perplexed.

"And what has that to do with me?" he asked.

She stared back.

"The Unfinished Sword," she replied. "It is the last hope. It, and it alone, can restore the Flame Wall. It must be returned to its original home. Until then, Escalon can never be safe."

He stared back, surprise in his face.

"And where is its home?" he asked, as the men crowded close to listen.

"In the north," she replied. "In the Tower of Ur."

"Ur?" Alec asked, baffled. "Has the tower not already been destroyed?"

Lorna nodded.

"The tower, yes," she replied. "But not what lies beneath."

She took a deep breath as they all looked to her, riveted.

"The tower holds a hidden chamber, deep below the ground. It was never the tower that was important—that was a diversion. It was what lay below. There, the Unfinished Sword will find its home. When you return it, the land will be safe, the Flames restored for all time."

Alec took a deep breath, clearly taking it all in.

"You want me to journey north?" he asked. "To the tower?"

She nodded.

"It will be a treacherous journey," she replied. "You will find foes on all sides. Take the men of the Lost Isles with you. Sail up the Sorrow, and do not stop until you reach Ur."

She stepped forward and placed a hand on his shoulder.

"Return the sword," she commanded. "And save us."

"And you, my lady?" Alec asked.

She closed her eyes and felt a terrible rush of pain, and she knew immediately where she had to go.

"Duncan dies as we speak," she said. "And only I can save him."

CHAPTER SEVEN

Aidan rode across the wasteland with Leifall's men, Cassandra on one side, Anvin on the other, White at his feet, and as they galloped, raising a cloud of dust, Aidan felt overjoyed at his sense of victory and pride. He had helped achieve the impossible, managing to redirect the falls, to change the massive rush of Everfall, to send its waters gushing across the plains and flood the canyon—and save his father just in time. As he approached, so eager to be reunited with his father, Aidan could see his father's men in the distance, could hear their shouts of jubilation even from here, and he felt filled with pride. They had done it.

Aidan was elated his father and men had survived, the canyon flooded, overflowing, thousands of Pandesians dead, washed up at their feet. For the first time, Aidan felt a great sense of purpose and belonging. He'd truly contributed to his father's cause, despite his young age, and he felt like a man amongst men. He felt this was one of the great moments of his life.

As they galloped, the sun shining down, Aidan could not wait for the moment when he saw his father, the pride in his eyes, the gratitude and most of all, the look of respect. His father would now, he was sure, look upon him as an equal, as one of his own, a true warrior. It was all that Aidan had ever wanted.

Aidan rode on, the thunderous sound of horses in his ears, caked in dirt, sunburned from the long ride, and as they finally crested the hill and came charging down, he saw the final stretch before them. He looked out at the group of his father's men, heart pounding with anticipation—when suddenly, he realized that something was wrong.

There, in the distance, his father's men were parting ways, and amidst them he saw a sole figure, walking alone in the desert. A girl.

It made no sense. What was a girl doing out there, alone, walking toward his father? Why had all the men stopped and let her through? Aidan did not know exactly what was wrong, but by the way his heart was pounding, something deep inside told him it was trouble.

Even stranger, as Aidan neared, he was floored as he recognized the girl's singular appearance. He saw her suede and leather cloak, her tall black boots, her staff at her side, her long light-blonde hair, her proud face and features, and he blinked, confused.

Kyra.

His confusion only deepened. As he watched her walk, saw the manner of her gait, the way she held her shoulders, he knew something was not quite right. That looked like her, but it was not. That was not the sister he had lived with his entire, with whom he had spent so many hours reading books in her lap.

Still a hundred yards away, Aidan's heart was pounding as he felt a deepening sense of apprehension. He lowered his head, kicked his horse and urged him on, galloping so fast he could hardly breathe. He had a sinking premonition, felt a sense of impending doom as he saw the girl near Duncan.

"FATHER!" he shrieked.

Yet from here, his cries were drowned out by the wind.

Aidan galloped faster, riding out ahead of the pack, racing down the mountain. He watched, helpless, as the girl reached out to embrace his father.

"NO, FATHER!" he shouted.

He was fifty yards away, then forty, then thirty—yet still too far to do anything but watch.

"WHITE, RUN!" he commanded.

White took off, running even faster than the horse. And yet still Aidan knew there would be no time.

Then he watched it happen. The girl, to Aidan's horror, reached out and plunged a dagger into his father's chest. His father's eyes widened as he dropped to his knees.

Aidan felt as if he, too, had been stabbed. He felt his entire body collapse within him, never feeling so helpless in his life. It had all happened so quickly, his father's men standing there, confused, dumbfounded. No one even knew what was happening. But Aidan knew. He knew right away.

Still twenty yards out, Aidan, desperate, reached into his waist, drew the dagger that Motley had given him, reached back, and threw it.

The dagger sailed through the air, spinning end over end, shimmering in the light, heading for the girl. She extracted her dagger, grimaced, and prepared to stab Duncan again—when suddenly, Aidan's dagger found its target. Aidan was relieved, at least, to watch it puncture the back of her hand, to see her shriek and drop her weapon. It was no earthly shriek, and certainly not Kyra's. Whoever she was, Aidan had outed her.

She turned and looked at him, and as she did, Aidan watched with horror as her face transformed. The girlish countenance was replaced by a grotesque, manly figure, growing bigger by the second, larger than any of them. Aidan's eyes opened wide in shock. It was not his sister. It was none other than the Great and Holy Ra.

Duncan's men, too, stared back in shock. Somehow, the dagger puncturing his hand had transformed the illusion, had shattered whatever magic sorcery he had used to deceive Duncan.

At the same moment White lunged forward, leaping through the air and landing on Ra's chest with his huge paws, driving him back. Snarling, the dog tore at his throat, scratching him. He clawed at his face, throwing Ra completely off guard and preventing him from rallying and attacking Duncan again.

Ra, struggling in the dirt, looked up to the heavens and shouted out words, something in a language Aidan did not understand, clearly invoking some ancient spell.

And then, suddenly, Ra disappeared into a ball of dust.

All that remained was his bloody dagger, fallen to the ground.

And there, in a pool of blood, Aidan's unmoving father.

CHAPTER EIGHT

Vesuvius rode north through the countryside, galloping on the back of the horse he had stolen after murdering a group of Pandesian soldiers—and on a rampage ever since, barely slowing as he tore through village after village, murdering innocent women and children. In some cases he passed through a village for its food and weapons; in others, just for the joy of killing. He smiled wide as he recalled torching village after village, single-handedly burning them down to the ground. He would leave his mark on Escalon everywhere he went.

As he rode out of the last village, Vesuvius groaned and threw a flaming torch, watching with satisfaction as it landed on yet another roof, setting another village aflame. He burst out of it with glee. It was the third village he had burned this hour. He would burn them all down if he could—but he had pressing business. He dug his heels into horse, determined to reunite with his trolls and lead them on the final stretch of their invasion. They needed him now, more than ever.

Vesuvius rode and rode, crossing the great plains and entering the northern part of Escalon. He sensed his horse tiring beneath him, but that only made him dig his heels in deeper. He cared not if he rode it to its death—in fact, he hoped he did.

As the sun grew long in the sky, Vesuvius could sense his troll nation getting closer, awaiting him; he could smell it in the air. It gave him great joy to think of his people here in Escalon, finally, on this side of the Flames. Yet as he rode, he wondered why his trolls were not further south by now, pillaging all of the countryside. What was stopping them? Were his generals so incompetent that they could accomplish nothing without him?

Vesuvius finally burst free of a long stretch of woods, and as he did, his heart leapt to see his forces spread out on the plains of Ur. Tens of thousands of trolls were gathering, he was thrilled to see. Yet he was confused: instead of looking victorious, these trolls looked defeated, forlorn. How could it be?

As Vesuvius watched his people just standing there, his faced flush with chagrin. Without him there, they all seemed demoralized, to have all the fight taken out of them. Finally, the Flames down, Escalon was theirs. What were they waiting for?

Vesuvius finally reached them, and as he burst into the crowd, galloping amongst them, he watched them all turn and look up at him with shock, fear, and then hope. They all froze and stared. He'd always had that effect upon them.

Vesuvius jumped down from his horse, and without hesitating, raised his halberd high, spun around, and chopped off his horse's head. The horse stood there for a moment, headless, then dropped to the ground, dead.

That, Vesuvius thought, *was for not riding fast enough.*

Besides, he always liked to kill something when he arrived somewhere.

Vesuvius saw the fear in his trolls' eyes as he marched toward them in a rage, demanding answers.

"Who is leading these men?" he demanded.

"I have, my lord."

Vesuvius turned to see a thick, large troll, Suves, his deputy commander in Marda, facing him, tens of thousands of trolls behind him. Vesuvius could tell that Suves was trying to look proud, yet fear lurked behind his gaze.

"We thought you were dead, my lord," he added, as if explaining.

Vesuvius scowled.

"I do not die," he snapped. "Dying is for cowards."

The trolls all stared back in fear and silence as Vesuvius clenched and unclenched his grip on his halberd.

"And why have you stopped here?" he demanded. "Why have you not destroyed all of Escalon?"

Suves looked back and forth from his men to Vesuvius in fear.

"We were stopped, my master," he finally admitted.

Vesuvius felt a rush of rage.

"Stopped!?" he snapped. "By whom?"

Suves hesitated.

"The one known as Alva," he finally said.

Alva. The name rang deep in Vesuvius's soul. Escalon's greatest sorcerer. The only one, perhaps, with more power than he.

"He created a fissure in the earth," Suves explained. "A canyon we could not cross. He has separated the south from the north. Too many of us have already died trying. It is I who called off the attack, who saved all these trolls you see here today. It is I you have to thank for their precious lives being restored. It is I who saved our nation. For that, my master, I ask that you promote me, and give me a command of my own. After all, this nation looks to me now for leadership."

Vesuvius felt his rage building to the point of explosion. Hands shaking, he took two quick steps, swung his halberd wide, and sliced off Suves's head.

Suves collapsed to the ground, while the rest of the trolls stared back in shock and fear.

"There," Vesuvius replied to the dead troll, "is your command."

Vesuvius surveyed his troll nation with disgust. He patrolled his lines up and down, staring into all their faces, instilling fear and panic in all of them, as he enjoyed doing.

Finally, he spoke, his voice sounding more like a growl.

"The great south lies before you," he boomed in his dark voice, filled with fury. "Those lands were ours once, pillaged from your forefathers. Those lands were once Marda. They stole what is ours."

Vesuvius took a deep breath.

"For those of you who are afraid to advance, I will collect your names, and your family's names, and I will have each one of you tortured slowly, one at a time, then sent to rot in the pits of Marda. Those of you who wish to fight, to save your lives, to reclaim what your forefathers once owned, will join me now. Who is with me?" he shouted.

There arose a great cheer, a loud rumbling through the ranks, row after row, as far as he could see, of trolls raising their halberds and chanting his name.

"VESUVIUS! VESUVIUS! VESUVIUS!"

Vesuvius let out a great battle cry, turned, and sprinted south. Behind him he heard a rumble like thunder, the rumble of thousands of trolls following him, of a great nation determined to put an end to Escalon once and for all.

CHAPTER NINE

Kyra flew on Theon's back, racing south through Marda, slowly returning to herself as she left this land of blackness. She felt more powerful than ever. In her right hand she wielded the Staff of Truth, light shining off it, engulfing them both. It was a weapon, she knew, that was bigger than her; it was an object of destiny, filling her with its power, commanding her as she commanded it. Holding it made the universe feel bigger, made her feel bigger.

Kyra felt as if she were holding the weapon she had been meant to wield since she was born. For the first time in her life, she understood what had been missing, and she felt complete. She and the staff, this mysterious weapon she had retrieved from deep in the lands of Marda, were one.

Kyra flew south, Theon, too, bigger and stronger beneath her, the fury and vengeance in his eyes matching her own. As they flew and flew, hours passing, finally the gloom began to subside, and the green of Escalon became visible. Kyra's heart leapt to see her homeland; she had never thought to see it again. She felt a sense of urgency; she knew her father, engulfed by Ra's armies, needed her in the south; she knew that Pandesian soldiers filled the land; she knew that Pandesia's fleets were pounding Escalon from the seas; she knew that somewhere high above the dragons circled, also bent on Escalon's destruction; and she knew the trolls were invading, millions of creatures tearing her land apart. Escalon was in dire straits in all directions.

Kyra blinked and tried to push from her mind the awful memory of her homeland torn to shreds, the long stretches of ruin and rubble and ash. And yet, as she clutched the staff tighter, she knew this weapon might be its hope for redemption. Could this staff, Theon, and her powers truly save Escalon? Could something so far gone be saved? Could Escalon ever even hope to return to what it had once been?

Kyra did not know. But there was always hope. That was what her father had taught her: even in one's bleakest hour, when things looked so grim, even if they appeared utterly destroyed, there was always hope. There was always some spark of life, of hope, of change. Nothing was never absolute. Not even destruction.

Kyra flew and flew, feeling her destiny well up within her, feeling a surge of optimism, feeling more powerful with each passing moment. She reflected, and felt she had conquered something deep within herself. She recalled slicing that spider's web, and she felt that, as she had sliced it, she had also severed something within her. She had been forced to survive on her own, and she had conquered the deepest demons within her. She was no longer the same girl who had grown up in Fort Volis; she was not even the same girl who had ventured into Marda. She returned now as a woman. As a warrior.

Kyra looked down through the clouds, sensing the landscape shift beneath her, and saw they had finally reached the border where the Flames had once stood. As she examined the big scar upon the land, motion below caught her eye.

"Lower, Theon."

They dove beneath the heavy clouds, and as the gloom dissolved, her heart lifted to see the land she had loved again. She was thrilled to see her own soil, the hills and trees which she recognized, to smell the air of Escalon.

Yet as she looked again, her heart fell. There, below, were millions of trolls, flooding the land, racing south from Marda. It resembled a mass migration of beasts, their rumble audible even from here. Seeing this, she did not know how her nation could ever withstand such an attack. She knew her people needed her—and fast.

Kyra felt the Staff of Truth buzz in her hands, then make a high-pitched whistling noise. She felt it calling her to action, demanding she strike. She did not know if she was commanding the staff, or if it was commanding her.

Kyra aimed the staff toward the ground, and as she did, a cracking noise emanated from it. It was as if she were wielding thunder and lightning in her palm. She watched in fascination as an intense orb of light shot forth from the staff and raced down for the ground.

Hundreds of trolls stopped and looked up, and she saw panic and terror in their faces as they looked at the ball of light coming down at them from the sky. They had no time to run.

An explosion followed, so powerful that its shock waves rocked Theon and Kyra even from the ground. The orb of light hit the ground with the force of a comet hitting earth. As it rippled, thousands of trolls fell, flattened by the ever-expanding waves of light.

Kyra examined the staff in awe. She prepared to slash it again, to wipe out the troll army—when suddenly, a horrific roar sounded above her. She looked up and was shocked to see the huge face of a scarlet dragon emerging from the clouds—and a dozen more behind it. She realized, too late, that these dragons had been looking for them.

Before Kyra could strike at them with her staff, a dragon reached out and swiped at Theon with its talons. Theon was caught off guard, and was sent spinning through the air by the tremendous blow.

Kyra hung on for dear life as they spun, nearly out of control. Theon's wings were upside down as he tried to right himself, and he turned again and again, Kyra barely hanging on, clutching his scales, until he finally straightened.

Theon roared in defiance and, despite being smaller than the bunch, he lunged upwards, fearless, at the dragon who had swiped him. The dragon was clearly surprised that the smaller Theon had rebounded, and before it could react, Theon sank his teeth into its tail.

The large dragon shrieked as Theon bit its tail clean off. It flew for a moment without a tail, then lost its bearings and plummeted, face-first, straight for the ground below. It landed with a crash, creating a crater and a cloud of dust.

Kyra raised her staff, feeling it burning in her palm, and swung it as three more dragons came for her. She watched as a ball of light shot forth and smashed the three dragons in the face. They screeched, stopped short in the air, then flailed. They became very still, then plummeted straight down, like rocks, until they, too, hit the ground with an explosion, dead.

Kyra was amazed at her power. Had the Staff of Truth really just killed three dragons with a single slash?

Kyra raised the staff again as a dozen more dragons appeared, and as she lowered it, expecting to fell them, she was suddenly surprised to feel a horrific pain in her hand. She turned and noticed out of the corner of her eye a dragon swooping down behind her, and its talons swiping the back of her hand. It slashed her hand, drawing blood, while in the same motion, it clutched the Staff of Truth and yanked it from her hands.

Kyra shrieked, more from the horror of losing the staff than from the pain. She watched, helpless, as the dragon flew off, taking the staff away from her. The dragon then dropped it, and she watched with horror as the staff tumbled through the air, falling end over end, down toward the ground. The staff, Escalon's last hope, would be destroyed.

And Kyra, defenseless now, faced a flock of dragons, all ready to tear her apart.

CHAPTER TEN

Lorna, feeling a sense of urgency, walked briskly through the camp, Duncan's men parting ways for her. Merk walked at her side, joined by Sovos and trailed by a dozen men of the Lost Isles, warriors who had forked off from the others and joined them on their journey out of the Bay of Death, back to land, and all the way out here, in the desert, past Leptus. Lorna had single-mindedly led them here, knowing that Duncan needed her.

As she approached, Lorna saw Duncan's men looking at her with wonder. They made room for her until she finally reached the small clearing where Duncan lay. Concerned warriors huddled around him, kneeling by his side, all gravely concerned for their dying commander. She saw Anvin and Aidan, weeping, White at their feet, emitting the only sound in the heavy silence.

A hand stopped her as she approached Duncan, and she stopped and looked back. Merk and Sovos tensed, hands on their swords, but she gently laid a hand on them, not wanting a confrontation.

"Who are you, and why do you come here?" Duncan's warrior asked sternly.

"I am King Tarnis's daughter," she replied with authority. "Duncan tried to save my father. I have come to return the favor."

The man looked surprised.

"His wound is fatal," the warrior said. "I have seen it many times in battle. He is past all healing."

It was Lorna's turn to frown.

"We waste time. Do you want Duncan to die here, bleeding? Or shall I attempt to heal him?"

The warriors were clearly all skeptical since their encounter with Ra and his sorcery, and they looked at each other. Finally, Anvin nodded.

"Let her through," he said.

They stepped aside, and as Merk and Sovos lowered their weapons, Lorna hurried forward and knelt at Duncan's side.

She examined him and knew immediately it was not good. She could sense the black aura of death around him, and knew, as she examined his closed, fluttering eyes, that the end was near. He was soon leaving this earth. Ra's blow had done grievous damage—not so much because of the dagger, but because, she sensed, of Duncan's feeling of betrayal behind it. Duncan still thought it was Kyra who had stabbed him, and she sensed in his aura that he no longer wished to live because of it. It was sapping his life force away.

"Can you save my father?"

Lorna looked over to see Aidan, red-eyed, cheeks wet with tears, staring up at her with hope and desperation. She took a deep breath.

"I do not know," she answered simply.

Lorna lay one palm on Duncan's forehead, and the other on his wound. She began to hum an ancient hymn, and slowly, the crowd fell silent. Aidan's weeping stopped. She felt a tremendous heat course through her palms, confronting his sickness. She closed her eyes and summoned all the power she had, trying to read his destiny, to understand what had happened, what his fate held in store.

Slowly, it all came to her. Duncan had been meant to die here today. That was his destiny. Here, in this place, on this battlefield, after his great victory in the canyon. She saw all the battles he had ever fought; saw his rise to warrior, to commander; saw his final and greatest battle here at the Canyon. He was not meant to survive the flooding. He was meant to die in its wake. He had taken the revolution as far as he was meant to take it.

She sensed his daughter, Kyra, flying through the air, on her way here, meant to take over his command. Duncan was meant to die at this moment.

Yet, as she knelt over him, Lorna summoned the power of the universe and begged it to change his fate, to change his destiny. After all, Duncan had been the one and only true friend to her father, King Tarnis, even when all others had turned his back on him. Duncan was the one her father had urged to come save her. For the sake of her father, she owed it to him. And she also, deep down, sensed that there might be within Duncan, still one epic battle left to be fought.

Lorna wrestled with fate, feeling the struggle exhaust her. She felt an battle epic of spirits raging within her, as she wrestled with powers she was not supposed to wrestle with. Dangerous powers. Powers that could kill her. Fate, after all, was not a thing to be taken lightly.

As she struggled, Lorna felt Duncan's life hanging in the balance. Finally, she collapsed in exhaustion, breathing hard, and as she did, an answer came to her: it was both victory and failure. Duncan's life would be extended—but only for a short while. He would be allowed one last battle, allowed to see his daughter's face

34

again, his *real* daughter, allowed to die in her arms. That, at least, was something.

Lorna shook, feeling sick, overwhelmed by the powers she had fought with. Her palms burned, and finally there came a flash, a feeling unlike any she'd ever felt, and she was thrown back by the power of it. She landed on her back a few feet away.

Merk quickly pulled her up, and she knelt there, weak, in a cold sweat.

A few yards away, Duncan lay unmoving, and Lorna felt overpowered by the magic of what she had summoned.

"My lady, what has happened?" Anvin demanded.

She struggled to clear her mind, to find her words.

In the silence, Aidan stepped forward and desperately confronted her.

"Will my father live?" he pleaded. "Please, tell me."

Lorna, passing out from exhaustion, summoned the energy to nod back weakly right before she did.

"He will live, boy," she said. "But not for long."

CHAPTER ELEVEN

Aidan was ashamed, yet try as he did, he could not help himself from crying. He had retreated to the far ends of the camp, to a cave on the outskirts of the field, hoping to be alone, not wishing for the other men to see his tears. Only White sat at his feet, whining beside him. He wished he could stop his tears but he could not, overwhelmed with grief over his father's injury.

He will live, but not for long.

Lorna's words echoed in his head, and Aidan wished he could erase those words. He would give anything for his father to be able to live forever.

Head in his hands, Aidan sobbed quietly. He replayed in his head the moment when Ra, disguised as his sister, had stabbed his father. Aidan had been galloping down the hill, had thrown a dagger, and had prevented Ra from stabbing him a second time. Yet, still, it had been but a moment too late. Why couldn't he have arrived a few minutes earlier?

Aidan blamed himself. If only he'd ridden faster, perhaps his father would not lay dying right now. Aidan felt that he was just reaching the age where he and his father could understand one another, as father to son, and as man to man. And yet just as he was beginning to know him, his father had been snatched away from him.

It was unfair. Aidan was too young; his father was too young; it was not supposed to be this way. His father was supposed to rise, to free Escalon, to become its new King, and Aidan was supposed to be there, by his side. Aidan had already seen it all happening in his head, had seen them moving back to the capital, had seen his father's coronation, his new legion. Who would be the King now? Who would be the new commander now? Who would lead the Escalon forces now? What would life in Escalon look like without his father?

Aidan felt completely lost without his father, adrift, especially in the wake of the loss of his brothers. Kyra was the only family he had left now.

"Your father still lives, boy," came a voice.

Aidan looked over, and was ashamed to see Motley and Cassandra enter the cave, a few feet away. They had clearly sought him out wishing to console him, yet seeing them only deepened his shame and guilt.

Aidan blinked back with bloodstained eyes.

"Did you not hear Lorna's words?" Aidan snapped, harsher than he wished to be. "He lives but for a short while."

Motley stepped closer.

"Yet he lives *now*," Motley insisted, one of the few moments Aidan had ever seen him serious. "And *now* is all we have. We live in dangerous times. You might die on this day, and I might as well. Your father is lucky to at least have another chance."

"And that is because of you," Cassandra chimed in, stepping close and holding his wrist. "You threw the dagger. You saved him. You and that dog of yours."

At his feet, White whined, licking Cassandra's hand.

"You should be very proud," she concluded.

Aidan shook his head glumly.

"I was too late," he replied.

Aidan did not want them to see him like this. He was a warrior now, after all, and this was not how warriors should behave. He wished he could be stronger.

His father was his rock, the one person he looked up to, whom he admired most in the world. Even more, his father was the strongest man he knew, stronger than all these great warriors. If he could die, then any of them could. Including Aidan. And that struck Aidan to the core. It changed the way he looked at the world. It even changed the way he viewed life: fleeting, cruel, tragic, without warning—and supremely unfair.

Justice, Aidan felt, had not been served. Why should an evil creature like Ra be able to even touch a fine man like his father?

"It's not *fair*," Aidan said, overwhelmed with grief.

Motley sighed, coming over and sitting with his great bulk on the rock beside him.

"True, young Aidan," Motley replied. "You finally get to see a glimpse of what life is about. Life is unfair. No one—*none* of us— is born with an assurance of a fair life. You will find that many more things in your life will happen which are unfair. The question isn't whether these things will happen to you, because they will. The question, rather, is: how will you will react to the injustices in your life? Will you cave in and let them consume you? Will you become bitter, cynical, self-pitying? Or will you remain strong? Will you fight back at the injustices, the unfairness of life?"

Motley sighed.

"Life's unfairness must be fought back against, daily, just like any foe. And most of that fighting must happen internally. You must never fold. And you must search for fairness even in the face of great unfairness. *That* is what makes a warrior."

Aidan slowly stopped crying as he considered Motley's words. He felt, deep down, that they were true, even while he resisted them.

"Yet there is supposed to be *justice* in the world," Aidan insisted. "You commit a crime, you get punished. You are good to others, they are good to you. Is that not how the world is supposed to work?"

Motley slowly shook his head.

"Life may show us *glimpses* of justice. But the vast majority of it, you will find, will be unruled, unregulated, and unjust. You must create your own sense of justice and act from it. Not because the world is just—but because *you* are just. After all, you are a microcosm of the world. You cannot prevent what the world shall give to you. But you can control yourself."

Aidan pondered his words in the long silence, sensing their truth.

"My father was fair and just," Aidan replied, calmer now, hollowed out. "And yet where did that get him? He ended up being treated unjustly."

"Your father *is* fair and just," Motley corrected, "and he was treated unjustly. That is true. But don't you see? It does not take away from the life he has led. He led a life of justice. And no single act of injustice will ever strip that from him."

Motley laid a hand on Aidan's shoulder, and Aidan turned to him.

"Dwell on the injustice of life, and you will only create more of it," he concluded. "Ignore it, and act justly yourself, and you will create a life of justice."

Aidan considered Motley's words, his tears gone now, as he began to see the truth in them. Cassandra reached over and held his hand, and he looked back at her. Her eyes were brimming with tears as she stared back.

"I love your father as the father I never had," she said softly, sadly. "He may die before his time, yet he lives right now. Cherish your time with him. I never had a father. You still have more time, in your brief window, than I ever had. Do not give in to self-pity. There are many people, like myself, who have it worse than you."

Aidan took a deep breath and felt foolish, realizing she was right.

"Be strong," she added, "for him. He needs you now. His fate has been written. Now you must decide what to do. Will you collapse? Or will you be at his side?"

Slowly Aidan felt a calm arise within him. He felt a new sense of purpose, of determination. And he began to feel a new desire.

For vengeance.

Aidan stood, wiped away his final tear, and felt cold, strong inside. He knew that something had shifted within him. He knew now that he was no longer a boy, but a man. A man who would soon be without a father. A man who would need to stand on his own two feet, and to avenge him.

It was time to leave boyish ways behind.

"It is time to go," Aidan said, taking that first step, "and avenge my father."

CHAPTER TWELVE

Seavig galloped west, leading hundreds of warriors of Esephus, determined to fulfill Duncan's command and wage war against the Pandesian fleet. He knew the odds were stacked against him and that the battle at sea would likely end in his death, yet it gave him no pause: it was the honorable thing to do for his country. And for Duncan, he would do anything.

As Seavig rode he thought of the vast numbers of the Pandesian fleet, and he knew this would have to be the most brilliant battle he and his men had ever waged at sea. He lived for times like this, times when his back was to the wall, when the odds were bleakest; he thrived when the situation demanded that he be not just a great warrior, but a crafty one as well. He was, after all, a man of the sea, and one needed great cunning to survive in the face of a storm.

The great stronghold of Esephus had stood for thousands of years because he and his fathers before him had managed to make it stand, had found a way to keep it alive, even exposed as it was to attack on the seashore. They were water people, and water people learned to move like the water, to rise and fall, to duck and weave. Water, after all, could flow even over the biggest rock in the world, and that was because it was malleable.

Seavig cried as he kicked his horse, urging him faster. Their destination, the western shore of Escalon, was but a short ride now, due west of Baris. It was the perfect place to enter the water, to begin the sail north, sail up the Sorrow, and eventually outflank the fleets of Pandesia. Where he was riding was a place no Pandesian would guard; it was not a town, or city, or stronghold. It was but a shoreline. It was nowhere, a coast uninhabited for hundreds of miles.

Seemingly uninhabited. There were no great strongholds or cities or even towns in this area, and the Pandesians would not guard the area. That was precisely the way this harbor was designed. For in times of greatest war, the ancient Escalonites wanted a hiding place in reserve. It was the secret place, known only to the commanders of Escalon, where the River Tanis met the Sorrow. Somewhere north of the Lost Temple and south of Ur, in the middle of seemingly nowhere, a secret meeting point had been designated for times of national emergency. It was a place where Escalon's sailors could rendezvous for battle, could take to the seas to save their homeland. Esephus, a great water city, was a natural target, and Seavig had designated a backup plan in case his city was taken. When Pandesia was closing in, he had sent one of his commanders to lead dozens of men to await him in the great caves of the western shore, where they could hide for months and not be found. It was there Seavig had stashed a dozen of his finest ships for times of war. Times like this.

Seavig prodded his horse, galloping faster, leading his men ever west, and as the sun grew heavy they finally burst through the thick wood, riding alongside the gushing River Tanis. Somewhere up ahead, he knew, it met the Sea of Sorrow. They would sail north, under the cover of darkness, along the coast, to Ur, and ambush the much greater Pandesian fleet. He would be outnumbered a thousand ships to one, yet Seavig had no fear. He went where battle called him.

They crested a hill, and finally, the sky opened and Seavig was relieved to see his great love in life: the ocean. There were the vast, rolling waves of the Sorrow, the sun shining off it, but a few hundred yards ahead. Even from here he could hear the great gushing of water, and he looked out and followed the Tanis and saw where all of its tributaries finally met the sea, gushing out in a great flood. It was a sight that restored his heart. When he saw water, he knew he was home again.

Seavig lowered his head, kicked his horse, and completed the final stretch. He and his men soon reached the great caves of the sea, and as he rode alongside the enormous rock, fifty feet tall, he quickly dismounted. His men followed him as he walked toward the caves, dwarfed by the soaring, arched entrance.

Seavig entered the dimly lit cave, and as he did, his heart soared to see hundreds of his men awaiting him inside. They all sat around a fire, swords in their hand, brooding, and as Seavig and his men waltzed in, they all stood. Their eyes filled with hope. Seavig was elated at the sight of the small fleet he had stashed away here for times of trouble. They floated inside the cave, in the tributary that flooded it from the sea, creating a perfect canal for the anchored boats to hide.

All his men at once stood and rushed toward him. His commander, Yuvel, was the first to embrace him. Seavig embraced him back, then embraced his other men, so happy to be reunited with them all again. Here were two hundred of his finest warriors, the finest sailors of Escalon, all back together again, all ready to wage war any way they could.

As his men finished embracing, they all gathered around and looked to him, and he commanded their attention.

"Warriors," Seavig boomed. "The fate of Escalon rests on our shoulders. Without securing our ports, without securing our shores, our land shall always be vulnerable. Our men on land look to us to hold the sea. Without the sea, the men of Escalon shall always be slaves."

Seavig looked out at all the faces, all looking back intently.

"Pandesians have taken our beloved city of Esephus, have destroyed our great water ports," he continued. "And now it is time for us to take it back. They have murdered countless of our brothers; now is our time to avenge them."

His men let out a cheer.

"We shall sail now," Seavig continued, "under the cover of darkness, north, along the Sorrow, to attack a thousand ships, to free Ur, and to liberate our ports once again. We shall confront a great fleet, and we shall likely not survive."

He looked out at all his men.

"Who is with me?" he called out.

As one, all his men cheered, and Seavig's heart lifted. There were true warriors.

Without another word they all quickly boarded the waiting ships. Seavig jumped to the bow of the first, and without hesitating, turned, raised his ax, and severed the rope tying it down.

The men cheered as his ship was immediately picked up by the great currents sucking it out to sea, into the Sorrow, into the twilight. Ur awaited them.

And the battle that would define their lives.

CHAPTER THIRTEEN

Kavos, flanked by Bramthos, led his hundreds of warriors north, riding for Kos, watching the mountains on the horizon as they neared Andros—determined to carry out Duncan's mission. Kavos brooded on the battle before him. He would have to find a way, as Duncan had commanded, to take on the northern Pandesian legion. It was no easy feat. He would have to lure the massive Pandesian army out from Andros, force them to attack him, to follow his men to Kos. If he was victorious, northern Escalon would be free of Pandesians; if not, his homeland would never be free, even if Duncan met victory at the Devil's Gulch.

Kavos knew this was a foolhardy mission. He, with his mere hundreds of men, could not hope to defeat a well-trained army of tens of thousands. In some ways, this was a death march. Yet Kavos had one glimmer of hope: if he could draw them away from the capital, if he could lead them all the way to the mountains of Kos, then they would be in his territory. It was an unforgiving territory for those who did not know it well—and Kavos and his men knew it better than anyone. There, high up in the mountains, he had men on reserve for a time like this. And if the stars aligned, maybe, just maybe, they could lead the Pandesians into a death trap.

Kavos rode faster, determined. He had not taken on this mission to save his own life, or the lives of his men; he had taken it in order to do what was best for his country, what his homeland demanded of him. If there was any hope of defeating these Pandesians, this was it. After all, the Pandesians would hardly expect an attack. A surprise attack might just stun their army, and in the chaos, they could make a rash decision.

Kavos kicked his horse and pushed him faster, riding as he had for hours, and as the sun began to set, finally, he saw it. It was at first, a faint image on the horizon, but as he neared, his heart leapt as he spotted on the horizon the outline of what remained of the capital of Andros, and the Pandesian forces lined up before it. There they were, milling around the city like ants, tens of thousands of men, holding the north, terrifying Escalon into submission.

Kavos was inflamed with rage at the sight of these invaders in his homeland, and especially his capital. The men of Kos, ensconced in the mountains, were separatists, yet they were still men of Escalon. And an indignity to Escalon was an indignity to them all.

"Horns!" he cried.

Kavos's men raised battle horns up as they rode and sounded them, one at a time, until the sound filled the sky. Slowly, the tens of thousands of Pandesian soldiers turned, spotting them as Kavos hoped.

Now that they caught sight of him, Kavos turned and led his men to the northeast, skirting the city, heading for the distant peaks of Kos. This was not the place to engage them, not here, in the open field; rather, he wanted to lure them away, to a place in which they be at a huge disadvantage. The question was: would they be foolhardy enough to take the bait?

Kavos looked back and his heart raced to see the Pandesians mount their horses, sound their own horns, and follow. He grinned, satisfied, as tens of thousands of men rode out of the capital, pursuing Kavos and his men toward the snowy mountains of Kos.

Kavos galloped faster, leading his men through narrow passes, between outcroppings of rock, zigzagging in the already snowy terrain, knowing he could not afford a single mistake. They had to reach the mountains before the Pandesians could reach them; otherwise they would be finished.

He rode and rode, thrilled to hear the rumble of an army chasing him, and he looked behind him to see the Pandesians closing in. They were gaining speed, and their forces outnumbered his own a hundred to one. Kavos turned and looked forward and saw the mountains looming. It would be a race to the finish.

He made a sharp turn between another narrow pass, and when he emerged, he was stunned at what he saw before him: there was another Pandesian garrison, blocking his path. He had not expected this. Thousands more Pandesian soldiers, on horseback, blocked his way to the mountains. He had underestimated them. The Pandesians must have known all along that he would come this way.

There was no time to stop, or to turn back—Kavos had no choice but to lead his men into battle against the much greater force. He lowered his head and charged and let out a great battle cry as he drew a sword and raised it high. Bramthos drew his sword beside him, as did all his other men, none, he was proud to see, slowing. They all thundered as one for the enemy, knowing they would have to fight their way through them if they had any chance of making it home.

Perhaps, Kavos realized, he would never reach his beloved mountains. Yet at least, he thought, as he lunged for the first man, he would die for his homeland in one final burst of glory.

CHAPTER FOURTEEN

Vesuvius led his nation of trolls south, storming the countryside, racing for the remains of the Tower of Ur. He heard their great shouts behind him, and took satisfaction in known his entire nation was reinvigorated now that he was leading them again.

Vesuvius held his halberd high, elated to be leading again, and let out a great battle cry. He could already see up ahead the fissure in the earth, the gaping chasm Alva had created which had swallowed up thousands of his trolls. Vesuvius watched as, in the distance, many of his trolls toppled trees, forming a temporary bridge to span the great divide. He watched as dozens attempted to race across it. Yet as they did, Alva merely widened his fissure, and the trees fell into the chasm along with dozens more screaming trolls. It was a slaughter.

Vesuvius scowled, more determined than ever. From here on in, the slaughter would end. There was only one way to defeat a powerful sorcerer like Alva, he knew. Not by sheer force—but through deception.

"TROLLS!" he shouted. "FOLLOW ME!"

His army followed as Vesuvius, but a few hundred yards away from the fissure, veered left instead of toward it. No, Vesuvius would not attack Alva head-on; that was a battle he could not win. He would go around him, instead, take the long way, and in the meantime ravage all the villages in his path. He could abandon the Tower of Ur for now, and circle back to it from behind, when Alva least expected it.

That was not all. Vesuvius could fight magic with magic. He could summon his own sorcerer, too, to create the cover for them they needed.

"Magon!" he shouted.

Magon, his prized sorcerer, rushed forward, running beside him, his head obscured by his scarlet cloak and hood.

Vesuvius pointed to the fissure, knowing what he wanted, and Magon shook his head.

"Magic too powerful for me, my lord," Magon said, anticipating his request. "I have tried many spells—yet I cannot seal it. I cannot conquer Alva."

Vesuvius scowled.

"Fool!" he snapped back. "I do not need you to conquer him. I need you to *distract* him. Send forth the red mist. Obscure our people in it, and obscure his vision."

Magon's eyes widened, clearly admiring the idea, and he turned and ran off. Vesuvius watched as he rushed to the edge of the fissure, then stopped and raised his shriveled, blackened palms to the sky. His wretched, malformed face was revealed as he leaned back and his hood fell, displaying rows of small, rotted, sharpened yellow teeth.

Magon snarled and his hands shook as small orbs of red mist arose from them and filled the sky. They rolled toward the fissure, and spread out, like clouds, creating a thick red mist.

Vesuvius grinned. This was precisely the cover he needed in order to obscure his approach from behind. He let out a shout and dug his heels into his horse as he led his trolls south and east, skirting the fissure, keeping his sights instead on a distant village. He felt the world rush by beneath his feet, and he raised his halberd and felt the thrill of imminent mayhem and murder.

Moments later, he tore through a village unannounced and unexpected, bursting down its dirt main street. Hundreds of villagers were milling about this small isolated village on the outskirts of Ur, as yet untouched by the Pandesians. There would be plenty of time to defeat Alva, Vesuvius knew, to circle back behind him. Now it was time to let the red mist work, and let Alva's power drain.

In the meantime, he could have his fun, could find murder elsewhere. Vesuvius did not even slow as he tore through the village, kicking up a cloud of dust amidst screams of villagers, panicking to get away. His first victim was an old man. He had barely turned around when a look of horror spread across his face. Vesuvius grinned. He lived for looks just like those. It was a look of shock. Of terror. Of the end of life.

Vesuvius swung his halberd and brought it down with such might that he chopped the shrieking old man in half.

All around him the villagers took note, panic in their eyes. Vesuvius could see they wanted to run. But of course, there was no time.

His trolls swarmed the village like locusts, swinging halberds, chopping humans as they tore through like a plague. Vesuvius, loving it all, was soon covered to his elbows in blood, and he let out great bursts of laughter.

Oh, how good it was, he thought, to be alive.

*

Kyle raised his staff and swung with both hands as fast as he could, smashing trolls left and right as they began to cross Alva's fissure. He and Kolva, fighting beside him, were the front line of Escalon's north, the two of them holding back the nation of trolls while Alva maintained the fissure. At his feet, Leo snarled, attacking trolls on all sides, helping to keep them at bay. Kyle wondered if Duncan and all the men down south had any idea of all that they were doing to keep their homeland safe.

Alva stood to the side, eyes closed, still humming, still widening the fissure, sending trolls, with their makeshift tree bridges, deeper and deeper into the chasm. It was a remarkable feat, and Kyle was in awe of him. Yet as he watched, he could already see Alva beginning to weaken, his arms lowering, and he realized he could not hold the fissure much longer. At the same time, too many trolls were slipping through, felling trees which functioned as bridges, leaving Kyle and Kolva to fight them back.

Kyle stepped forward and smashed a troll who leapt off a log spanning the fissure, sending him back down into the earth. Several more sprinted across another tree they had felled, and they all landed around Kyle before Alva could widen it, surrounding him.

Kyle jumped into action, swinging and cracking one in the jaw, jabbing one in the solar plexus, and then coming up from under another one and smashing him in the chin. One troll grabbed him from behind, shockingly strong, and Kyle heard a snarling and turned to see Leo land on his back and clamp down on his neck. The troll shrieked and backed off, Leo wrestling it down to the ground.

Kyle turned and kicked as another troll approached to tackle him, knocking him back with such force that he sent him flying back into the fissure with a shriek. Another troll leapt from behind and swung a halberd for Kyle's back. Kyle ducked low, allowing the blade to swing overhead, then spun, grabbed the troll from behind and threw him. He watched as the troll stumbled and fell, shrieking, into the fissure.

Kyle fought like a man possessed, spinning and striking every which way, feeling the very defense of Escalon to be in his hands. The air filled the perpetual cracking noise of his staff as he felled soldiers in every direction.

Yet suddenly, in mid-swing, Kyle found his vision obscured; he blinked, confused at what was happening, groping before him. The world was turning red.

A thickening fog rolled toward him, making it impossible to see. He could hear thousands of trolls, snarling, charging, and he could hear the horns of the nation of Marda being sounded. He thought for a moment he spotted Vesuvius, leading some of his army in another direction, circling around, and he could not understand what was happening.

Beside him, Kolva paused after smashing two trolls back into the fissure, and squinted suspiciously into the mist.

"What is happening, my lord?" Kyle called out to Alva.

Alva stood there, eyes closed, pausing, before he replied.

"Vesuvius plans a great treachery. Soon enough they will reach us."

"What shall we do?" Kyle asked.

Alva opened his eyes for the first time, light shining from them, his face filled with urgency.

"The Flames must be restored," Alva finally said. "That is the only way."

Kyle and Kolva exchanged a baffled look.

"But how?" Kolva asked.

Alva closed his eyes for a long time, then finally opened them again.

"Within the Tower of Ur," he began, "deep beneath the earth, lies the chamber of secrets. Within it lies our only hope."

Kyle blinked back, confused.

"The tower, my lord?" he asked. "But it is destroyed."

Alva turned to him, his eyes so intense he nearly had to look away. It was like staring into the sun.

"What you see is only rubble," he replied. "The real secret of the tower lies not in its stone, but in what lies beneath."

Kyle stared back, shocked, then turned and examined the massive pile of rubble where the Tower of Ur once stood.

"The tower rises high," Alva continued, "yet it extends even deeper beneath the earth. The Tower of Ur was never a decoy. Each tower held its own great secret. Ur's secret never resided above ground—but below."

Kyle looked back, awestruck. He had never known of the tower's secret.

"You must find it," Alva urged him. "Clear the rubble and find the chamber. We cannot hold these trolls for long. That chamber is Escalon's only hope."

Kyle looked again at the rubble, at the hundreds of trolls clamoring over it in the descending mist, and he knew that reaching it would require an epic battle. Yet he had no choice: it was life or death.

Without hesitation, Kyle bounded off, raised his staff high, and threw himself into the midst of the troll army, Leo at his side, fighting for all he had, determined, even at the cost of his life, to find the lost chamber—and rescue Escalon.

CHAPTER FIFTEEN

Duncan led his thousand warriors on horseback, galloping west across the plains of Baris, heading for the Devil's Gulch, and as he rode, he felt like a changed man. Still recovering from his wounds, he felt weaker now than he had ever been—in fact, Lorna had urged him to stay back and rest until he was fully recovered. Of course, he could not. He had an army to lead and a war to wage, and he knew that time would not wait for him.

Duncan rode in his weakened state, one hand on the reins, the other clutching his chest, blood still seeping where Kyra had stabbed him. Of course, he had to remind himself, it was not Kyra who had stabbed him, as much as she had looked like her—it was Ra, with his sorcery. Yet still the vision haunted him, his own daughter stabbing him, the idea of its being her hurting him more than the actual event. He could not shake the image from his head, and that, after all, was the real damage that Ra had done.

Duncan also could not shake from his mind another vision he'd had—that of his dying. He had felt his body getting lighter, crossing to the other side, and he could remember the moment of his leaving, his body so light, his ancestors awaiting him on the other side. He recalled an intense sense of peace and comfort he could not shake. He had been leaving, he felt certain of it, when King Tarnis's daughter had brought him back.

Returning had been painful. He remembered blinking, looking up into Lorna's face, the awful pain in his chest. The experience haunted him. He did not know what was scarier—leaving this world or returning to it.

It was all the more scarier when he had been told by Lorna, upon returning, that he had but a short lease on life left. He was defying his destiny, being given one final opportunity for battle and glory, one final chance to resolve the loose ends of his life. He was riding now on the final stretch of life, he knew, whatever little of it was left, and he was determined not to squander it.

Duncan rode and rode, the galloping of horses filling his ears, along with the sound of armor and weaponry clanging from his hundreds of men behind him. Anvin rode at his side, Aidan, Motley, and Cassandra behind them, White at their feet, and as Duncan reflected on his men, he took pride in knowing that he had dispatched them to the corners of Escalon to end this war, Seavig to the western shore to liberate Ur, and Kavos to the north to battle the legions near Kos. With everyone doing their part, they would have a chance, even if remote, to liberate Escalon once and for all.

Duncan's forthcoming battle in the Devil's Gulch, he knew, would be the riskiest of all.

Duncan shouted and kicked his horse, gaining speed, determined to stay out in front of his men despite his pain, determined to lead by example and show his men that he was strong. He coughed up blood as he rode and wiped it away furtively with the back of his hand, not wanting any of them to see how sick he truly was.

Duncan gazed out at the horizon, taking stock. He knew that Ra's army would be heading south now, coming to find him, and indeed, as he looked back over his shoulder, he could already see, on the distant horizon, an endless line of black forming, Pandesian banners blowing in the wind. This time they would not come at him with ten thousand men, but a hundred thousand, all of Ra's forces, a vast and terrible army all bent on Duncan's destruction.

Duncan rode and rode, increasing his speed, knowing they didn't have much time if they were to make it in time to prepare a defense. In the distance he could see the shape of the Devil's Gulch beginning to form, the towering cliffs rising a hundred feet high, jagged. The gulch they formed was wide enough only to accommodate a few men at a time, the greatest bottleneck in all of Escalon. It was his only hope, he knew.

If Duncan could lure Ra through the narrow passageway comprising the Devil's Gulch, with its steep cliffs on one side and its raging sea on the other, he could stand a chance. He had to find a way to get Ra's entire army to pass south through the gulch, then seal it up. Duncan hoped they would take the bait, and sensed that they would. Indeed, their rumbling only grew louder behind him, and he knew an army that big, with bait before it, pumped up with bloodlust, would never stop for anything. Their hubris, if he was right, would lead to their downfall.

As the sun fell lower in the sky, each step of the horse hurting Duncan so much that he clenched his jaw at the pain, he and his men finally reached the Gulch. They all came to a stop, and as they did Duncan turned and searched the horizon: the Pandesian army had not, to his relief, called off the pursuit. Indeed, they were closer now.

Duncan's men, stopped amidst a cloud of dust, breathing hard with their horses, turned and looked at their leader, and he could feel all their eyes on him. He turned and surveyed his men, hiding his pain, knowing they needed strong leadership now more than ever.

"Volen!" he commanded.

Volen , one of his trusted commanders and one of the oldest of the bunch, stepped forward, at attention.

"You will remain on this side of the Gulch and lead the bulk of our men. You will take cover beneath the caves and wait for the Pandesians to pass through. You shall then seal the Gulch and bar them from reentering Escalon."

"And you, my lord?" Volen asked, concern in his eyes.

"I shall lure the Pandesians through the Gulch, so you can close it off behind us."

Duncan could see all of his men looking back at him, concern in their eyes. A thick, somber silence fell.

"But then how shall you return, Commander?" Volen finally asked.

Duncan shook his head slowly.

"I may not," he replied. "I will lead them far enough, then circle back and attempt to pass back through the caves in these cliffs, if I do not find them sealed. If I can, I shall reunite with you here. If not, you shall seal up the Gulch either way."

They all stared back, grim-faced, the silence so thick, nobody stirred.

"Father," came a voice.

Duncan looked over to see Aidan, standing close, looking back up at him, tears and pride in his eyes, White at his feet.

"I shall come with you," Aidan said.

Duncan was touched by his son's courage. Yet he shook his head firmly.

"You shall stay with the bulk of the army here." He then turned to the others. "I shall not ask any of you to join me, given the risk of this mission. Whoever wishes to volunteer, can."

With that, Duncan kicked his horse, turned, and rode off toward the Gulch, having no time to lose, and expecting to ride alone.

Yet to his surprise, there soon arose a thundering of horses behind him. He turned and saw Anvin, joined by dozens of his men, all riding with them. He was touched by their loyalty.

"HORNS!" Duncan cried, issuing the first command.

No sooner had he uttered the words when his men sounded dozens of horns. Glancing back over his shoulder, Duncan was pleased to see the Pandesian army following, closing in, like a snake to a flute, all thundering for the Gulch.

The greatest battle of his life, he knew, lay but moments away.

*

Aidan stood with the bulk of his father's soldiers beneath the towering cliffs of the Gulch, Motley and Cassandra at his side and White at his feet, all hiding in the recesses of the caves as the thunderous Pandesian army roared by. Aidan's heart sank as he watched them, as he thought of his father riding through the Gulch. He knew it was a heroic mission, one from which he might never return. He watched the tens of thousands of men roar past, like a river without end, and his foreboding only deepened. Was this the time in which his father was destined to die?

It appeared as if the tides of the world were coursing by, and Aidan had no idea how his father could ever defeat them. Yet he also had a sense of relief. The final epic battle for the fate of Escalon had come. It was their ultimate chance to face Pandesia once and for all, to live or to die as free men—but no longer to cower in fear.

Aidan fidgeted, itching for action, no longer able to be still as he watched.

"I want to go out and fight them," Aidan said to the others. "I want to be by my father's side."

Cassandra shook her head.

"You will only get us all killed," she chided, grabbing his arm. "You cannot go out there and fight them now. Your father has chosen his fate. You will wait with the rest of us and help seal the gulch when the time comes. We shall be safer here, anyway, on this side."

He frowned.

"I do not wish to be safe," he replied.

Aidan could not stand the idea of his father out there, and he waiting here. It burned within his small warrior's heart, a great yearning to assist his father in any way he could.

Unable to take it any longer, he finally drew his sword and took a step forward, prepared to enter the fray, as reckless as it may be.

Suddenly, he felt a strong, reassuring hand on his wrist.

"There is another way. A smarter way."

Aidan turned to see Motley looking down at him, his expression grave.

"Deception trumps might any day," Motley continued. "To defeat your enemy, do what he expects least."

Aidan furrowed his brow.

"And what is that?" he asked.

"Join him."

Aidan stared back, confused.

"Join the Pandesian army," Motley added. "In disguise. Be the worm from within. That's where you can do the most damage."

Aidan pondered Motley's words. They made sense. It was a bold plan, sneaking behind enemy lines—and he liked it.

"But how?" Aidan asked.

"The tunnels."

Motley gestured to the shadows, and Aidan looked and saw, in the dark recesses of the caves, small passages burrowed into the cliffs.

"They lead to the other side," Motley added. "You could emerge on the other side, steal armor from an unsuspecting soldier, and slip into their ranks. You could join them on the chase for Duncan, wait for your moment, and help him when he needs it most."

Aidan grinned broadly, loving the idea. Here, finally, was something he could do.

Aidan wasted no time: he jumped into action, rushing forward, deeper into the shadows, heading for the tunnels. Outside, he heard the thunderous roar of the Pandesians racing by.

He heard a noise and looked over to see Motley at his side, and Aidan stared back with wonder.

"You're coming?" Aidan asked.

Motley grinned, yet beneath it, Aidan could see him sweating.

"Can't let you die alone, young friend."

Aidan heard the draw of a sword, and looked over to see Cassandra standing at his other side.

"Nor I," she added.

He heard a snarl, and looked down to see White at his feet, joining them, and he stood there, so grateful for all his friends' loyalty.

"You first," Motley said. "You're smaller."

Aidan grinned back. "Who are you calling *small*?" he retorted.

Motley smiled and Aidan stepped forward, crouched low, and stepped into the black dampness of the tunnel, hoping beyond hope that it let him out on the other side—and into the thick of the Pandesian ranks.

CHAPTER SIXTEEN

Kyra plummeted through the air, clinging to Theon's back, as they spun wildly out of control. She saw the ground rushing up to meet them, knew she would be dead in a few moments, and yet despite that, she wasn't worried for herself. She could think only of one thing: that Staff of Truth. There it was, far below her, tumbling end over end, dropping through the sky as it fell toward the ground, gleaming each time it caught the light.

Kyra could scarcely believe that dragon had snatched it from her hands. She had felt so powerful, so invincible, had been certain that she and the staff would never be separated. And just like that, in one single swipe, the fate of Escalon, so fragile, was reeling; her own destiny, so precarious, was in jeopardy. How was it possible? How could a dragon's swipe get in the way of destiny?

The more she dwelled on it, the more Kyra began to realize that destiny was fragile. Fate was fragile. True, what was meant to be was meant to be; yet she also had to intervene in her destiny if she were to shape it. As she fell, Kyra also realized something else: the staff was testing her. It was testing her strength, testing her resolve. Was she truly worthy of wielding it? It was forcing her to become bigger, stronger than herself.

Kyra closed her eyes and tuned into the energy of the staff and slowly, she realized that she and the staff were truly one. That nothing could come between them. She began to realize that the space between them was just an illusion. That there was no such thing in this world as separation.

In a moment of sudden insight, Kyra thrust out her palm and allowed that to come to her which she knew she deserved to have.

Kyra felt a tremendous wave of heat shoot through her body, her palm feeling as if it were on fire, and as she looked down, her heart leapt to see the staff suddenly reversing course. It suddenly flew upward in the air, right for her—and a moment later, it stuck to her palm.

As it did, Kyra felt alive again, felt more powerful than she'd ever been. Nothing could separate them now.

Kyra pulled up on Theon, and they leveled out just feet before hitting the ground, so close to trolls below that their swinging halberds nearly touched them. Then they ascended once again. Kyra looked up and kept the dragons in her sights, and she and Theon, equally determined, flew right for them.

As they reached the flock, Kyra swung the staff. The lead dragon dove for her, massive, with thick, red scales, and an orb of light emanated from the staff and stopped it in its tracks. It shrieked, stopped cold, and then suddenly, dead, plummeted straight down. It landed far below with a tremendous crash, crushing a hundred trolls beneath it.

Emboldened, Kyra swung the staff overhead in a wide circle, while Theon flew higher, gaining momentum, aiming for the next dragon. This one had huge, green scales, and as Kyra swung the staff, she smashed its throat, sending it rocking to her side, then tumbling end over end down to the ground below. It landed with a tremendous crash, dead.

Theon flew higher, as Kyra felt the staff urging them on. She let out a battle cry and leaned forward to face the three yellow dragons diving down for them. Theon, fearless, opened his jaws and lunged forward and clamped down on the throat of the one in the middle. The dragon screeched, wrestling with him.

The other two closed in, and Kyra swung the staff, smashing one in the head with such force that she sent it hurtling backwards, then smashing the other across its back, sending it flipping end over end, screeching as it fell down to the ground, dead.

Theon still wrestled with the much bigger dragon, clamping onto its throat despite the bigger opponent scratching and biting him. Kyra, jerked back and forth as Theon struggled, raised her staff with both hands and brought it down straight between the eyes of the dragon opposite her. White sparks flew everywhere, and the dragon screeched, released its grip, and dropped like a stone straight down to the ground below. There followed a distant boom as the dragon hit the ground, creating a massive crater and sending up huge plumes of dust.

Kyra and Theon threw themselves into the rest of the flock, and one at a time, they destroyed each and every dragon, the Staff of Truth felling them like a thing of wonder. Finally there remained but two dragons still flying. They approached, and Theon bit the tail of one of them, swinging it wide, then sending it hurtling sideways. The other dragon, though, approached too quickly, opening its mouth to breathe fire and kill them both.

Kyra had little time to react. She raised her staff and instinctively threw it. It flew through the air and landed in the dragon's throat, just as the flames came out. The Staff of Truth stopped and then reversed the flames, and as it did, it consumed the dragon in a ball of flame.

As the dragon began to plummet to its death, Kyra raised her palm and summoned the staff. It came back to her, unscathed, saved before the dragon's jaws closed. The massive beast, the final dragon, dropped down to the ground, shrieking in a great ball of flame.

Kyra, breathing hard, was thrilled to realized they had won. Theon was bleeding and bruised, looking for more dragons, yet as she flew, she was amazed to see there were none left. She looked down and saw all the dead dragon carcasses littered below, and she realized with a shock she had killed Escalon's remaining dragons. Finally, the skies above Escalon were free.

Kyra turned to fly south, eager to find her father—when suddenly there came an awful shriek, reverberating in the skies. She peered into the horizon, wondering where it had come from, and what it could possibly be.

It is they, came a voice in her mind's eye.

Kyra looked down and realized Theon was talking to her in her mind's eye.

"Who?" she asked.

When all the dragons are dead, the Great Ones will arise. The four great dragons from the four corners of the earth. They have been awakened.

The awful shriek came again, and as it did, Kyra felt herself fill with despair. She knew, even from so far away, that they were coming, and that the battle she had just fought would be nothing next to what was to come.

CHAPTER SEVENTEEN

Seavig led his fleet in the black of night, sailing up the Sea of Sorrow, and the tension grew thick on the silent ship as they neared the port of Ur. Seavig's heart beat faster as he spotted the sprawling Pandesian fleet, thousands of ships, black silhouettes against the sky, seeming to fill the entire sea. They had the harbor of Ur surrounded, and as Seavig looked out at the city, his heart hurt to see they had flooded it. It was a port he'd remembered fondly, and its destruction felt like a knife in his heart.

Yet the loss of Ur was not his immediate concern; he was focused, instead, on the much greater numbers of the Pandesian fleet. How could his mere dozen ships, he wondered, attack a fleet of thousands? On the face of it, all was hopeless.

Yet during the long sail up here he had been pondering a plan. It was a plan that required stealth, surprise, and the cover of night, in order to do what no sailors had ever achieved before. Seavig had learned as a boy to make do with what he had—that, his father had taught him, was what won battles. And this fleet was all he had, and he was determined to make it work.

They sailed closer, Seavig willing his men to be silent, the only sound audible that of the waves lapping against the hull and the tense breathing of his men. All his men were in position, awaiting his command as they sailed forward, the tension so thick that he could hear his own heart pounding. His ship, leading the way, floated through the harbor, hardly a hundred yards away from the closest Pandesian ship.

If he had one saving grace, Seavig knew, it was that the Pandesians would never possibly expect an attack. Their ships bobbed there, unsuspecting, their sailors fast asleep, the only sound in the blackness the groaning of their ships in the water, the creaking of their ropes. It was just as Seavig had hoped.

They sailed closer, and closer, Seavig's heart pounding, knowing all his men were looking to him and knowing he needed to wait as long as he could before executing his plan. He had primed them on the way up, and any moment it would be time to execute it.

"NOW!" Seavig finally hissed.

His men all jumped into action. His dozen ships quickly came together, sailing beside one another until their hulls touched. His men quickly threw ropes and grabbed them, ship to ship, yanking them tight to secure all the ships in his small fleet to one another, as one floating mass. Once the ships were secured his men ran across the decks, jumping from one ship to the next, abandoning the ships one at a time and all crowding onto Seavig's ship. Seavig could feel his ship getting heavier as they did, sinking a bit with the weight of it, protesting, yet still staying afloat.

Soon, of his dozen ships, only one held his men; the other eleven sat empty, as he had planned.

"CUT THE ROPES!" he commanded.

A group of men jumped from one ship to the next, quickly in the night, chopping ropes. As they did the ships began to separate, while the men quickly returned to Seavig's ship. They all stood there and watched as the ships slowly drifted apart.

Seavig turned and looked ahead, up at the looming hull of the Pandesian warship before him, and nodded to his men. As one, they all soundlessly charged, rushing across the deck, then, as they reached the bow, jumping on board the Pandesian warship.

Seavig led the way. They all moved stealthily across the much bigger Pandesian warship, raising daggers as they raced through the ship and slicing the throats of the sailors standing guard. They felled them quickly, holding their mouths, preventing the enemy from making a sound. Seavig knew that if even one cried out, all would be lost. With each slice, each man he dropped, he thought of vengeance for Escalon.

Within moments, the dirty work was done. His men killed everyone on board, sparing no one, per Seavig's command. He could not take the chance, outnumbered as they were. They had taken over the entire ship, not a sound uttered, and Seavig turned and looked anxiously to the rest of the Pandesian fleet, hoping no one had spotted them. He was relieved to see they had not.

He breathed with relief. The first step of his mission, and perhaps the trickiest, had been accomplished. They had commandeered a much larger Pandesian warship, and had set their own fleet adrift. Now there was no time to lose.

"ARROWS!" he hissed.

His hundreds of men raced to the ship's rail, took a knee, and lined up as they drew the bows from their backs.

"FLAMES!" he hissed, as he took a knee and joined them.

He and his men pulled arrows from quivers and touched torches to them. Within moments, a thousand small points of light filled the night.

"FIRE!"

As one, his men all placed their arrows and fired.

The night sky filled with thousands of small points of light, arrows aflame, sailing in a high arc, silently through the night. Their course was not set for the Pandesian fleet, though—it was, rather, set for Seavig's ghost fleet.

Seavig watched as the small fleet he had sailed here with was suddenly set aflame. The ships continued to drift toward the greater Pandesian fleet, aflame. The flames grew higher, roaring as they ate up the sails, the masts, and soon the ghost fleet became a weapon, a floating wall of fire, unstoppable, heading for the much greater Pandesian fleet.

Seavig watched with great satisfaction as his fleet of fire did what he hoped it would. The first ship's hull touched a Pandesian warship, and within moments it set it ablaze, its flames licking its rails, deck, then climbing up the sails. The dozen other ships followed suit, some hitting Pandesian warships directly but most brushing up against them just long enough to set them aflame, then continuing to sail, setting more and more ships aflame.

Seavig watched, his eyes aglow, as the night was lit up. Shrieks soon rang out, of surprised men being awakened, burned alive, men stunned by panic. There followed the sounds of splashing, as men jumped below, aflame, to their deaths in the sea.

Then, finally, the sound of bells tolling. And of a chorus of warning horns.

Chaos ensued as the huge Pandesian army began to wake, dozens of its ships aflame, the flames spreading on the steady wind with every passing moment.

Seavig's men all turned to each other and let out a great cheer.

The battle for Ur had begun.

CHAPTER EIGHTEEN

Merk stood at the bow of the small ship, Lorna beside him, sailing in the black of night up the western coast of Escalon. The Sorrow was still, eerily calm. All that was audible was the gentle splashing of tiny sea creatures jumping alongside the hull. Merk looked down and saw them swimming alongside their ship, following it, lighting up the night with their fluorescent scales as they glowed beneath the water. Merk found himself getting lost in their brilliant colorful patterns, and he felt as if the entire sea were following him.

Once again Merk found himself on a ship with Lorna, and again, he found himself overcome by his feelings for her. He had never truly felt close to anyone in his life, had never taken comfort in anyone's presence, but with her, it was different. After all, she had saved him back there, in the Bay of Death; without her, he would surely be dead by Vesuvius's hands. No one had ever saved him before—or even cared about him.

Lorna's mystery only deepened for Merk when he watched her heal Duncan on his deathbed in Baris. It had been miraculous to watch, and made him wonder even more about her powers. When Duncan had recovered and had asked Lorna to head north, to aid in the battle of Ur, she had selflessly accepted the duty. Merk had insisted on accompanying her, and she had not resisted.

Was it because she liked him? he wondered. Was it because she felt for him as he did her? Or was it only because she needed the company in the pending battle?

"You have barely spoken," Merk said to her, wanting to break the silence, eager to know more about her, to establish some connection with her.

Lorna glanced at him, and her glowing blue eyes, looking gray in the night, captivated him as always.

"You know we sail into the entire might of the Pandesian fleet," he added.

She nodded back knowingly, and he was surprised to see her unfazed.

"Yet you are unafraid?" he asked, eager to understand her.

She shook her head, and he could see that she was not. It only deepened her mystery.

"Death has never held fear for me," she said, her voice as soft and mysterious as the twilight. "Only not living with purpose."

He wondered.

"But your powers," he said, needing to know. "With your powers, can you stop an entire army?"

"No," she admitted. "I cannot."

His heart sank. He had hoped that she was secretly confident of their victory, yet he could see from her face that she was not. The death sentence awaiting them seemed ever more certain. And yet, as this was where they were needed, neither of them would let their country down.

"Duncan does not need two more bodies to die with him at the Devil's Gulch," she replied.

"Would you rather die up here, in the north, in the blackness of the ocean?" he asked.

She smiled.

"Where else would you propose?" she asked.

He shrugged, nervous to say what he was really thinking.

"Maybe…" he began, his voice tremulous, "we can forego this war."

Lorna turned and stared at him, her eyes widening in surprise, and Merk felt his throat go dry. He wondered if he had gone too far.

"Forego?" she asked.

He hesitated. Then, finally, he summoned the courage.

"Just you and I," he continued, softly. "Leave. Somewhere…away from all this. After all, what good will two more dead soldiers do in this war?"

"And abandon our homeland?" she asked, and Merk felt himself sinking. Perhaps he had made a mistake to ask.

He shrugged.

"Our homeland has abandoned me many times," he said. "I care far more about you than I do about it."

She stared back, and he could see she was grappling with her thoughts, her feelings. He plunged forward, knowing he had gone too far, and it was now or never.

"Not every battle is ours to fight," he continued, speaking it all in a rush. "I love Escalon. But I love life more. My entire life has been one of shifting loyalties. Most of all, loyalty to myself. To survival. To the highest bidder. I want to live now. Finally, I know what I want from life, and I want to live with you. Let's get away from all this," he said, stepping forward and taking her hand. "Let's be together."

A long silence fell as she stared back, seemingly stunned. Merk felt his hands shaking in hers; he had never felt so nervous.

Finally, she looked away and removed her hands, and as she did, he was crestfallen. His heart pounded, as he wondered. Had he gone too far in revealing his feelings? What if she did not feel the same for him?

Suddenly, he felt stupid, feeling sure that she did not. He wanted to curl up and die, to be anywhere but on this ship.

Finally, she spoke, her voice soft in the night.

"My father served as king," she said. "And his father before him. Loyalty to our homeland runs in my blood. I am sorry, Merk. This land, this war, is all I have."

She still did not speak to his proposal, though, did not speak to her feelings for him and he wondered if he detected anything in her voice.

"And there is nothing that will change your mind?" he asked, tentative. "Not even I?"

She looked away, and he felt foolish.

"You are a fine man," she said. "Finer than you know. You have done dark deeds in your life, yet I understand you—you have lived a life of survival. I suspect inside you there is a yearning for more, a yearning for a cause. Yet what I have learned is that we survive not by thinking only of ourselves; we survive through our *causes*. Through looking out for *others*. Through a purpose bigger than ourselves. That is what it means to be alive. Otherwise, we are not truly living."

Merk pondered her words as the two of them slipped back into an interminable silence, the only sound that of the splashing of the waters against the hull. The silence engulfed them for hours as they sailed ever north. The wind picked up, sails flapping, adding to the chorus, carrying them into the distance.

Shoulders slumped, Merk retreated into himself, feeling rejected, feeling more baffled by her than ever. Most of all, he felt ashamed. Something in her words had rung true. He had indeed always looked out for himself, for his own survival. Perhaps she was right. Perhaps the key to survival had been lying, all this time, somewhere outside of himself.

Yet he felt conflicted. Merk was not scared of dying; he just did not want to die for other people's causes. He would rather die in his own way, in his own place, his own time. The life of a soldier had never meant anything to him, and Escalon had never looked out for him. Why should he serve it?

Hours passed as the silence grew thicker, the blackness more absolute, the stars shining. Merk found his eyes growing heavy, and he had nearly fell asleep when he heard a soft gasp.

He looked up, eyes heavy with exhaustion, to the water before him. Lorna stood there, gripping the rail, and as Merk saw what she was looking at, he, too, stood up straight. Now he was fully awake.

The picture before him made no sense: there, on the horizon, the sea appeared to be aflame. He looked closely and saw the silhouette of thousands of Pandesian ships surrounding Ur, and saw dozens of these aglow. Men were shouting orders, distant from here, and some ships fired cannons. Chaos and confusion ensued. It appeared the Pandesians were under attack.

"Seavig has begun his attack," Lorna finally observed, shattering the silence.

She turned to him.

"Our time is now."

She turned the wheel and Merk saw her set their direction for a massive Pandesian ship, its sails rising nearly a hundred feet high. He spotted hundreds of soldiers in the boat, staring north into the flames, none of them looking south, down at the waters, none expecting a tiny ship like this to creep up on them.

"And now?" Merk asked Lorna, his foreboding deepening. "Are we attack this fleet alone?"

"A battle begins with one ship," she replied calmly.

Merk looked at her firmly.

"Are you mad?" he asked, exasperated. "Do you really expect we can defeat that entire ship of soldiers yourself?"

She smiled back.

"No," she replied. "I expect you to."

He blinked, stunned.

"I, against a hundred men?" he asked.

"You have your dagger," she replied, "and your speed. That is all you need, when I create cover for you."

"Cover?" he asked.

She stared back, intense.

"You have to trust me," she replied. "If you are willing. Are you ready to serve your country?"

Merk stood there, feeling at a crossroads. He had never truly cared for a cause before. Yet when he searched Lorna's eyes, he recognized a fierceness in them, one that made him want to serve her cause, whatever it should be.

He finally straightened and stared back at Lorna, resolute.

She saw the look of approval in his eyes, and she turned and raised two palms to the sky, closed her eyes, and leaned back.

As she did, Merk watched in amazement as a white mist began to come forth from her palms, filling the air, filling the night. It wrapped itself around the ship like a snake, creeping down to the water and slowly, steadily, spread across the sea and to the Pandesian fleet. Within moments, the night was thick with her fog, so thick, he could not even see past the rail.

At the same moment, their small ship bumped gently into the hull of the massive Pandesian warship. Merk, heart pounding, knew the time had come.

Merk reached out, grabbed the long rope dangling down the side of the ship, and jumped, hanging on as he slammed into the hull. He yanked himself up one inch at a time, palms burning and not caring.

Ten, twenty, thirty feet he climbed in the fog, straining from the effort, until he finally reached the rail. He grabbed it and looked down; already the rope was lost below in the thick mist.

Merk hung there, by the rail, took a deep breath and steeled himself. This was his moment. He knew that as soon as he crossed that rail he would encounter an army of hostile men, all wanting his death. It would be the most deadly battle of his life. One wrong move and it would be over.

Merk's heart slammed in his chest as he finally pulled himself over the rail, landing lightly with his two feet on the deck. He turned and was relieved to see he was, at least, immersed in a wall of fog so thick he could barely see his own hand. Lorna was good to her word: he had cover.

Merk wasted no time. He drew his dagger and rushed forward, using his killer instincts to find soldiers, darting from one to the other, slicing throats left and right as he went. He grabbed men's mouths before they cried, silencing them.

Still, their bodies dropped with thuds, and a commotion ensued on deck as the others caught wind of a killer amongst them.

Yet Merk gave them no time to react. He darted from soldier to soldier, killing each. A few turned to catch him, but Merk moved quicker and faster than all of them, doing what he did best, what he was born to do, using his dagger with mastery and speed and stealth, as he had always done on behalf of the kingdom.

There was little they could do against an invisible foe, a trained assassin. Within moments, the ship fell very still, Merk standing there, breathing hard, covered in blood.

It took a moment for the realization to sink in: this Pandesian warship was theirs.

Merk heard a noise behind them, a light thud, like a cat landing on deck, and he turned to see, out of the mist, Lorna emerging.

Merk sheathed his dagger, while she stepped forward, drew hers, and sliced the rope anchoring the ship.

Merk felt the massive ship begin to move beneath them.

He turned to her, wondering.

"Now what?" he asked.

"Now," she replied, smiling, "we sail into battle."

CHAPTER NINETEEN

Dierdre and Marco rode on the back of Andor in the black of night, heading south, away from the ruins of the Tower of Ur, away from the battle still raging with Alva and Kolva and Kyle, and determined to spark a battle of their own. Dierdre peered into the blackness as they rode, eager to return to her former city of Ur, even if it was now under water. She was eager to avenge her father.

Dierdre tried to collect her thoughts as she rode, still in shock at everything that had happened. She had been so sure, when she had set out with Marco for the Tower of Ur, that they would find Kyra there, that they would find safe haven together and have a chance to start again. She had never expected to find the tower destroyed, to find trolls attacking it, had never expected to find herself immersed in the front lines of an epic battle to spare the north. She had, most of all, never expected the Flames to be lowered, Escalon to be overrun. It had been like leaving a nightmare to walk into hell.

She would have surely died there had it not been for Kyle showing up, saving them—and then Alva appearing on his heels and saving all of them. Alva's command to ride to Ur was one she had been too happy to obey. She could not wait to leave that place. Dierdre still saw in her mind's eye the grotesque faces of the trolls, lunging for her, trying to tear her apart, and she wanted to get as far away from them as she could.

The idea of being able to be of service in her home city consumed her. She and Marco had had no choice but to flee Ur after the flood, yet now that they were returning, she was elated. If there was any glimmer of hope for her city to rise again, she would gladly give her life for it.

She wondered, though, what Alva had foreseen. She could not imagine, after the destruction she had seen, how her city could ever rise again. And she did not see how she and Marco could possibly offer any meaningful help. Yet, after witnessing his power she trusted Alva, and was all too eager to do her part to help.

Dierdre and Marco finally broke through the woods, she so hopeful for a glimpse of her city, praying that she would somehow find it rising from the waters. Yet as she did, she was dismayed at the sight before her. She had hoped that perhaps Alva had seen something she had not, that she might find an epic battle here that would see her city restored. Yet instead, she blinked, confused, as they stopped their horses and caught their breath.

There was nothing before them but water.

It was exactly as they had left it, the city of Ur now a lake, shimmering in the black of night, its harbor filled with thousands of Pandesian ships. There was no battle. It was in the same state of total conquest and defeat.

She and Marco exchanged a glance, both baffled, wondering why Alva had dispatched them here. Had he been wrong?

Dierdre peered out into the horizon, searching the black of night, wondering if she were overlooking something—and as she did, she saw something which caught her eye. There, on the horizon, far out at sea, she saw a dim haze of light; it appeared that some Pandesian ships were aflame. She was confused. Who could possibly be attacking the Pandesian fleet?

As she listened closely, she thought she could hear the distant rumble of cannon fire. She realized, with a jolt of hope, that a battle was raging. Someone was fighting back against the Pandesians.

"The war is beginning," Dierdre said excitedly. "We must help them."

She kicked her horse and they rode downhill, skirting the lake that was once Ur, her heart pounding, until finally they reached the shore where the harbor met the cliffs.

They stopped, breathing hard, and looked out. A battle was clearly raging. Cannons boomed, and cannonballs, she could see, sailed through the night, between rows of ships aflame. Dierdre wondered who was fighting.

She looked closer to her and observed the Pandesian ship anchored closest to the harbor. It was massive, its ropes tied near the cliffs, and on its deck she could see, lit by torchlight, Pandesian soldiers rushing across the deck, lighting cannons, their great wicks sparking. She suddenly reeled back as there came another boom, and she watched as a cannonball soared from the ship through the night.

Dierdre followed its trail out to the ocean and saw its missed target: a lone ship, sailing in the blackness, its silhouette visible amidst the conflagrations. It cut its way stealthily through the greater Pandesian fleet. Dierdre's heart skipped a beat as she realized: those were Escalon soldiers aboard that Pandesian ship. They had commandeered it. It was cutting through the fleet and wreaking havoc—and now the Pandesians were aiming to blow it to pieces.

"We must stop them!" Dierdre said urgently. "They will kill our people! We must board that ship and stop them from firing!"

"But how?" Marco asked.

Without waiting, Dierdre dismounted, ran, and took a flying leap off the cliff. Her stomach plummeting, she aimed for the huge rope anchoring the Pandesian ship and just caught it, palms burning. She wrapped her legs around it and began to climb. Andor whinnied from land, as if egging her on, as if furious he could not join her.

The rope burned at her palms and the arduous climb made every muscle in her body ache. She inched her way up slowly, one foot at a time, making her way toward the edge of the ship, eager not to be seen. Luckily the Pandesian soldiers, their backs to her, were too fixated watching the battle at sea to check their backs.

Dierdre suddenly felt a great shaking on the rope, and she looked down to see Marco landing on it, following her lead and climbing too, just feet behind her.

She soon reached the rail, and in one quick move climbed over the edge. Marco was close behind, and as the two of them landed on deck, they both rose to their feet and looked at each other, shocked they had made it this far, that they were in the thick of enemy territory.

Andor, on land, clawed the ground, stomping, irate he could not join them.

"Go, Andor!" Dierdre called out, feeling badly for this great beast who had brought them here, not wanting him to give them away. "Return to Kyle. Fight for us there!"

Andor did as he was asked, turning and galloping off, needing no prodding.

Dierdre, heart slamming, saw, feet in front of her, dozens of Pandesian soldiers lined up at the rail, heaving cannonballs, preparing the cannons, and lighting torches. She looked out to sea and was able to finally see who they were firing at. She gasped in recognition.

"Seavig!" she whispered to Marco.

"You know him?" Marco asked.

"My father fought with his men many times," she replied. "We must help them."

She knew there was little time.

"But how?" Marco asked.

Dierdre gestured to Marco, and they both watched the soldiers lowering torches to the cannons. Without thinking, they both rushed into action at the same time.

They sprinted forward and as they reached the unsuspecting Pandesians, Marco tackled one to the ground, while Dierdre grabbed hold of the hair of another and yanked him away. She also snatched his torch and hurled it over the edge, sending it hissing into the water below. The cannon was already lit, though, and Dierdre, realizing there was no time, threw her body weight into it, desperate to move it before it fired at Seavig's ship.

Dierdre shoved it a foot to the right a second before it fired.

A great boom shook the air, and the cannonball flew through the air and just missed Seavig's ship, thanks to her.

The commotion on deck caught the attention of the other soldiers, though, and Dierdre turned to see dozens of fully armed, irate Pandesian soldiers charging for them. She realized, too late, that she had thrown herself right into the enemy's lap.

She had saved Seavig. But her run had come to an end.

*

Alec stood at the bow of the ship as he led the small fleet from the Lost Isles, gripping the Unfinished Sword and staring out at the Sea of Sorrow. It had been a harrowing journey from the Bay of the Death all the way along the cost, but finally they were nearing the harbor of Ur. They would skirt it, as was the plan, sail around the massive Pandesian fleet, and continue on in the darkness all the way to the Tower of Ur, where Lorna had directed him to go. It was where, she had said, the Unfinished Sword must be put to use to end this war, and Alec, loyal soldier that he was, would go anywhere he was needed to save his homeland.

Alec held the Unfinished Sword tight the entire way up here, gripping the hilt, unwilling to let it go, this magical weapon which had become a part of him. He marveled at how his life had changed since the Bay of Death. He still saw in his mind's eye his felling of dragons. It almost felt like a dream.

As they neared the port of Ur, this place that had once meant so much to him, Alec was overcome by a new feeling. He could not quite understand it, but it was almost as if the sword were communicating with him, as if it were urging him to stop here. As they approached the harbor, Alec held out a hand and the ship came to a stop, and the fleet behind him.

His men stood beside him, looking at him questioningly.

"Why have we stopped?" one of his men asked, coming up beside him.

"The Pandesian fleet lies ahead," another chimed in. "If we stay here too long, they will see us."

Alec gripped the rail and felt a vibration run through his palm from the sword's hilt.

"I sense something," he said.

He closed his eyes and felt the sword commanding him.

"I am needed here," he finally said.

The men looked at each other, baffled.

"Our mission is to bring you—and the sword—to the Tower of Ur," the soldier replied. "You heard Lorna. She told us not to stop for anything. It is too dangerous."

Alec nodded.

"And yet, I feel I am needed here now. I cannot abandon the cause the sword is leading me to."

The men looked to each other, baffled.

"If we stop here, we will all be killed," added another soldier, coming up beside them. "We have no time. We must sail from here, and along the coast to the tower of Ur. The Pandesian fleet will soon spot us."

Alec nodded, realizing.

"That is why you shall go on without me," he said, stepping forward to the rail, preparing to depart. "Sail north and meet me at the Tower of Ur."

The men looked at each other, then at him, shock in their eyes.

"You will die here," the soldier said sadly.

Alec shook his head.

"I go where the sword bids," he replied. "It shall protect me."

Without another word, Alec grabbed a rope and lowered himself down into a small dinghy. It rocked wildly as he sat in it, and he wasted no time in pushing off from the larger ship, rowing quickly.

Before him lay the entire fleet of Pandesia, and as he rowed, he realized he would be one man against a nation. As much as he wanted to, he did not look back. He knew he had to only look forward.

Alec rowed and rowed, cutting through water, alone in the small dinghy, feeling dwarfed by the midnight sky, the million red stars, and the enormity of the universe. He navigated his way silently through the Pandesian fleet, his only saving grace the impenetrable dark and a persistent mist that drifted in and out, thickening like a fog. His boat was too small, luckily, for the Pandesians to be looking for—if it were any bigger, he figured, he'd be long dead by now. He did not know where the Unfinished Sword was leading him, but he knew enough by now to trust his instincts.

Rowing for he did not know how long, losing track of time as he watched the changing of the stars, Alec finally sat up, alert. There, up ahead, he saw it. Ships were ablaze.

Alec soon found himself navigating amidst a burning Pandesian fleet, amazed at the size and scope of the fires, wondering what battle had happened here. He looked about in confusion as Pandesian horns sounded through the night, echoing in the fog; he marveled as he watched Pandesians battling each other, as if trying to get away from an invisible enemy. He wondered what had happened here, and he wondered why the sword burned hotter in his palm as it led him closer and closer to shore.

Finally, Alec spotted a single ship in the distance, and he sensed that was his destination. The sword was pulling at him, demanding he go there.

Alec rowed until he reached the hull of the Pandesian ship, and when he did, he leapt from the dinghy, grabbed the dangling rope and pulled himself up. Soon he was up over the rail, and as he landed on the deck, he did so at a run, the sword in hand, the weapon practically pulling him where he needed to go. He knew that doing so could mean his death, that he was throwing himself into the arms of the enemy, yet he trusted the sword.

Alec spotted soldiers up ahead, and he charged, raised the sword, and let out a battle cry. There was a mob of Pandesians, crowding around somebody, and as Alec charged, the mob turned and stared at him, shocked; as they parted ways, they revealed who was on deck.

To Alec's shock, he saw his old friend Marco lying there, along with the girl he loved, Dierdre.

He could not have been more surprised to see them—yet he did not pause. He could see in an instant that his friends were in danger. They lay prone on the deck, the Pandesians surrounding them, about to kill them.

Alec pulled back the Unfinished Sword, lunged into the crowd, and slashed. The sword emitted an odd humming noise as it sliced through three men at once, so fast that it cut them in half before they could even raise their swords. Alec then spun and slashed at another soldier's sword, and it sliced the metal in half; he then swung around and, with the hilt, knocked the man clear off the railing.

Alec spun again and again, cutting through the mob of soldiers, moving in a blur, the sword commanding him as if it were an extension of his arm. He swung and spun and slashed, untouchable, the sword humming through the air like a living thing. Men fell all around him, their cries ringing out, more than one knocked back over the rail, splashing into the depths.

Within moments Alec looked around and realized he was the last man standing there in the quiet. He breathed hard, taking it all in, amazed. He had killed them all. Dozens of dead soldiers lay on the deck—and he had hardly even realized what he was doing.

Alec looked up, remembering Marco and Dierdre. They rose to their feet, staring back at him with wonder and gratitude.

"Alec," Marco called out. He stepped forward and embraced his old friend, while Alec, slowly snapping out of it, embraced him back.

Yet even as he did, Alec felt numb. He turned and looked into Dierdre's eyes, and as their eyes locked, he saw something. It was an expression of love. But not for Alec. For Marco.

Immediately, he understood. Dierdre loved his friend now. Not him.

In his moment of realization, Alec felt as if he had been stabbed in the gut. He felt betrayed—by her, by him, by the world.

Dierdre stepped forward, tears in her eyes.

"I thought you were dead," she tried to explain. "You left us all."

Alec shook his head.

"I never left," he corrected. "I was fighting on another front."

"But…you did not tell us," she said, now seeming unsure.

"There was no time," he replied.

"Whatever it was, it is good to see you back, my friend," Marco said cheerfully, not realizing. "I missed you."

Yet there was no joy in Alec's heart now. Only sadness. Remorse. Betrayal.

He and Dierdre locked eyes, and he could begin to see the sadness and regret in her eyes, too. Slowly, he felt his world spinning out from under him. Seeing Dierdre again had been the only thing keeping him alive. Alec had never anticipated this, and seeing her here, in love with his best friend, was more than he could handle. He wanted to run, to be anywhere but here.

"You are safe now," Alec said, his voice dark, joyless. "The soldiers are dead. The ship is yours."

"What do you mean?" Marco asked, confused, holding out a hand as Alec stepped to move away. "Are you leaving us? You just arrived."

Alec could not bring himself to respond. His love for Dierdre overwhelmed him, as did his sense that he had lost his best friend. Without another word, he hurried for the rail.

"Where are you going?" Dierdre asked, rushing forward. He could hear the concern in her voice. That, at least, was something.

He turned and stared back at her, his eyes willing up.

"I must leave for the Tower of Ur," he said.

Her eyes widened.

"The tower is overrun with trolls," she said. "To go there would be to go to your death."

He looked back, unswayed.

"I am already dead."

Without another word he turned and leapt over the edge, into the dinghy, determined to never lay eyes on her again. He would like, actually, to die a lonely death. After tonight, life for him held nothing in it.

As he rowed, cutting through the waters, distancing himself from the ship, a single cry, a shriek, cut through the darkness.

"Alec!"

It was Dierdre, calling his name. She was crying as she called it. He could hear the sadness in her voice. It was a cry of love, of loss, of what could have been. He wanted more than anything to look back, to see her face one last time.

But he did not dare. Instead, he rowed and looked ahead, saying goodbye, in his mind, to her forever.

CHAPTER TWENTY

Kavos charged for the legion of Pandesian soldiers who blocked his way to the mountains of Kos, not stopping for anything, ready to fight to the death. How dare these Pandesians invade his homeland, dare to think they could defeat him on his own territory? Those mountains of Kos belonged to his people; they always had. And no invading enemy had ever managed to conquer them. After all, they were now in the land of ice and snow, the land which had stood apart in Escalon for thousands of years. It took a certain type of man to survive in a land of ice and snow—and the men of Kos had it coursing in their blood.

Kavos looked up and knew they had to reach those mountains if they were to have any chance of outrunning the Pandesian army pursuing from behind. These soldiers in his way had to be destroyed immediately.

"MEN OF KOS, CHARGE!" he yelled.

A triumphant battle cry sounded behind him as he and his hundred men tripled their speed, lowering their heads, preparing to battle the much greater force of Pandesians. Although outnumbered ten to one, they did not slow or hesitate.

Their fearlessness clearly caught the Pandesians off guard. They seemed shocked to see these warriors of Kos increase their speed instead of stopping and surrendering.

Kos felt ire rise up within him as he extracted a spear and leaned forward and hurled it. It whistled as it flew through the air, a thing of beauty, camouflaged with the snow and ice. It found its target in the chest of the Pandesian commander, and he grasped it with both hands with a look of pain and shock, as he dropped off the side of his horse, dead.

Kavos let out a great battle cry as he drew his sword, increased his speed, and threw himself into a group of soldiers. He slashed one across the chest, spun and stabbed another, then, in a surprise move, he leapt from his horse and knocked two more soldiers off of theirs.

He tumbled with them to the ground, then rolled over and slashed the legs of two horses charging him, sending their men to the ground as he rolled and stabbed each in the chest.

Kavos's men were equally ferocious, leaping from their horses, fighting with the fervor and intensity the men of Kos were known for. Bramthos used his shield as a weapon, smashing several soldiers in a whirlwind as he galloped through their ranks, knocking them from their horses. He then drew his sword and swung with both hands, dropping a half dozen soldiers with blows so mighty they sliced their armor in two. Kavos's other commander, Swupol, swung expertly with his flail, smashing a half dozen soldiers before them and creating a wide perimeter in the chaos.

All around him his men fought with a fury unlike any they'd ever known, their lives at stake, felling Pandesians in a blur of motion. As they swept through the unsuspecting Pandesian force, before long they had carved a path and nearly evened the odds, dropping the first two hundred Pandesians while losing very few of their own men.

Kavos, in the thick of it, fought even harder, leading the way, elbowing and head-butting and beating one soldier after another, dropping them, yanking them from their horses, stabbing them with swords and daggers, swinging maces and hatchets he swiped off the ground. He would do whatever he had to, to reach those mountains and keep his people alive.

And yet, as their initial charge petered out, Kavos soon learned that these Pandesian soldiers were made of tougher stuff. The rear lines fought fiercely, unlike their vanguard, while Kavos's men were beginning to tire.

At a stalemate, Kavos, fighting with both hands, shoulders tiring, knew there wasn't much time. Behind him, on the horizon, horns sounded and there came a distinct rumble; he knew the bulk of the Pandesian army was closing in. He could not fight them both off. He had to do something quickly.

Kavos knew the time had come to call in the reserves. Looked up at the mountains, he spotted a glistening of light, and he took heart, knowing his men, up high, were awaiting his return—and awaiting his command. The men of Kos had a rule they lived and died by: when their men set out for battle, an equal number of men had to always remain behind to protect the mountains of Kos. It was a sacred duty that they had pledged, and it was what it meant to be a man of Kos. The reflecting light was a sign that his other soldiers were up there, high above, watching, ready, willing, and able to help them.

Kavos knew the time had come.

He grabbed a horn and blew it in three short bursts, a signal only his people would understand.

"RETREAT!" Kavos shrieked to his men.

His men looked baffled, yet they listened, obedient soldiers that they were. They all turned and ran. As they did, the Pandesians, emboldened, let out a cheer. Kavos could feel them bearing down behind them, the enemy surely thinking that they had them.

Yet they did not know the men of Kos. The men of Kos never retreated—for any reason.

As they ran, behind them there arose a distant rumble, high up. It grew and grew. Kavos smiled, knowing what it was—yet the Pandesians were too focused on pursuing their enemy to stop and consider the men of Kos could have another plan. What they did not consider was that they could be attacked from above.

Kavos turned as the crash came, and he looked up to see massive boulders rolling down the steep cliffs of Kos, huge, rolling with a fury that only a few mountain ranges could allow. The men of Pandesia finally stopped and looked up. Panic spread in their faces—too late.

The avalanche of boulders landed with a sound Kavos would never forget—crashing down, shaking the earth, as if the entire world were fracturing. Within moments, they crushed hundreds of Pandesians and rolled over hundreds more. Their cries filled the air, as they were all flattened or wounded, with no room to escape.

Kavos stopped running, and his men turned and let out a cheer. With those men dead, they now had an open path to the mountains. And not a moment too late: closing in on them was the Pandesian army, hardly a few hundred yards away.

"TO THE MOUNTAINS!" Kavos cried.

They cheered, and all took off together. They galloped faster and faster, skirting the boulders, fleeing from the Pandesian army until they reached base of the cliffs. When they reached the point where it was too steep for the horses they dismounted and ran on foot.

Then they climbed the mountain. It soon became a steep hike, and then became a crawl. Without hesitating they all removed the ice picks from their boots, and soon the clinking of their chipping ice filled the air as they all climbed the steep mountain face, scaling the cliffs like goats.

Kavos heard a great commotion and glanced down to see the Pandesians closing in, reaching the base of the cliffs. They were hardly fifty yards away.

Yet fifty yards made all the difference. In these mountains, a fifty-yard climb made the difference between the men of Kos and all the others, between men who could climb on ice and men who could not. He watched as the Pandesians pathetically tried to climb, then slid back down, falling again and again down the steep face of the cliffs. They were only fifty yards away—yet it might as well have been a mile.

Out of reach, knowing they were untouchable now, the men of Kos let out a great cheer. They climbed with their ice picks higher and higher, back into their homeland, into the protective mountains of Kos, just out of reach of the army—and preparing to make the greatest stand of their lives.

CHAPTER TWENTY ONE

Duncan charged south, leading his men through the narrow pass of the Devil's Gulch, the wind in his hair, his heart racing as he knew this might be the final battle of his life. He let out a battle cry, inspiring his men behind him, all of them cheering with him as they tore through the narrow opening, cliffs on one side, the crashing sea on the other. Behind them came the thunderous rumble of a hundred thousand Pandesians pursuing, getting closer by the moment. It was like death charging for them. Duncan glanced back and saw they were now hardly a few hundred yards behind. They had taken the bait. As close as they were, one wrong move would mean his death.

As reckless as this maneuver was, Duncan had no choice. He had to lure the Pandesian army through the Gulch, to get them to ride to the southern side of the cliffs so that his men could seal and defend the Gulch. If he was lucky, he could circle back and slip through the tunnels and reunite with his men, join them in making a stand in the Gulch itself. If not, he would die here, on this side of the Gulch. Either way, the Pandesians would be lured from Escalon.

The Devil's Gulch, the most famed place of Escalon, the proving ground of the greatest warriors who walked this land, would have to be put to the test. There was no other way he and his few hundred men could make a stand against a hundred thousand soldiers.

Horns sounded every few steps, Duncan pleased to hear his men following orders, helping to lure the Pandesians through. The Pandesians did not even pause—yet Duncan did not expect them to; there were few commanders, he knew, who were disciplined enough to call off a hot pursuit to what seemed a certain victory. In his experience, armies with greater numbers always fell prey to the trap of bloodlust.

As Duncan rode, he thought of the remainder of his army left behind on the far side of the Gulch, hundreds of great warriors hiding deep in the cliffs, waiting for the Pandesians to pass. They would seal the Pandesian army out of Escalon once and for all, trapping them on the other side of the impassable wall of mountains. Of course, in the process, they would seal Duncan out, as well. Duncan was willing to make that sacrifice, to take a chance and see if the hidden passages tunneling beneath the mountainside would lead him back to the other side and allow him to reunite with his men. His chance of survival was slim—and untested. Yet it was the chance he had to take. After all, it was the only way to save his homeland.

Duncan was relieved as he and his men finally burst out of the gulch, into the open field and sky, out of the narrow pass and onto the other side. It was great to be out in open daylight again, out from the claustrophobic confines of the Devil's Gulch. He charged south, all his men shouting, blowing horns, raising clouds of dust. They were the liberated shouts of men who were riding to their deaths, and who had nothing left to lose.

Now that they'd cleared the other side, Duncan's first impulse as a soldier was to turn around, to circle back for the hidden tunnels, and ride back to safety. Yet as a commander, he knew he could not. He had to lead the Pandesian army deeper, to make sure they all followed him south, through the gulch. He could not take a chance and turn back too soon, even though every passing second increased his chance of death.

"RIDE!" he shouted to his men, giving them inspiration, all of them knowing that each step increased their likelihood of death. Duncan led by example, riding faster, farther south, farther away from the cliffs, from their only salvation. And all of his men did, too.

Duncan began to hear the intense rumble behind him that could only mean one thing: the Pandesian army had broken through the Gulch. He glanced back and saw he was right. A hundred thousand warriors began bursting out, their ranks widening. It was awe-inspiring, like watching a river burst through a dam. Duncan had fought in epic battles, yet he had never seen so many soldiers amassed in one place in his life. It was like the might of the world bearing down on him.

"FASTER!" he shouted.

Duncan could feel the apprehension rising amongst his men as they rode farther from the gulch, from safety. He rode until his breathing grew heavy, feeling the shooting pains in his chest where he had been stabbed; he reached down and felt fresh blood, and knew the wound was not healing. Yet there was no turning back now. Not when his people needed him.

Duncan rode and rode until finally he glanced back and saw the Gulch was now distant on the horizon, and that the entire army of Pandesians had passed through. His mission had been achieved—now the time had come.

"TURN!" he shouted to his men.

His men turned with him, as one, following his lead as they all made a broad turn to the left. They turned in a wide arc heading back for the cliffs. He could not ride straight back, as he wanted to, or else he'd run right back into the Pandesian army. So instead he led his men in a broad arc, gradually back toward the cliffs. It was a risky move, exposing them to attack from the side, leaving one flank unprotected. Yet he had no choice if they were to make it back.

Sure enough, within moments, the first assault came. Pandesian horns sounded, and the sky suddenly filled with arrows raining down on his men.

"COME TOGETHER!" Duncan cried, expecting this. "SHIELDS!"

His men raised their shields and came in close that they formed a wall of iron, nearly touching shoulder to shoulder as the first volley of arrows hit. They came in so tight that there was nowhere for the arrows to penetrate—they merely bounced off the shields with a great clanging noise.

Duncan, sweating, lowered his shield with the others and continued riding in a broad circle back toward the cliffs, widening the arc, trying to get away from the forking Pandesian army. He had a head start on them but it was slim, barely a hundred yards, and narrowing.

Duncan saw the Pandesians raising their bows again.

"SHIELDS!" he cried.

Again, his men came together and raised their shields, and again they blocked the volley of arrows, bouncing off their shields as if it were raining down iron. Yet Duncan heard one of his men cry out, and he turned and saw Bathone, a proud young warrior who had volunteered, who had grown up with his sons, fall from his horse, an arrow in his side. An arrow had slipped through. As he fell, Duncan could tell he was still alive. He desperately wanted to stop for him, but he knew he could not. To do so would mean the death of all his other men. It was times like these that he wished he was not a commander, but a mere soldier once again.

Duncan saw the Pandesians closing in and realized the cliffs were still too far; he knew he had to do something desperate to increase their speed if they were to make it.

"DROP THE SHIELDS!" he shouted.

His men looked back at him, baffled, yet, disciplined as they were, they did not hesitate to follow his command. They threw down their heavy shields and as they did, they all kicked their horses, following Duncan's lead, and increased their speed. They needed speed now, more than anything, Duncan knew, if they had any chance of beating these Pandesians back to the cliffs.

Duncan lowered his head, kicked his horse, and charged with all he had. With the imposing granite cliffs in sight, he rode faster and faster, faster than he had ever ridden in his life, ignoring his pain, his wound, he and his men fueled by adrenaline, by the knowledge that they could die at any moment. Duncan could hear the Pandesians firing arrows again behind him, and he braced himself, knowing that if they reached him, exposed as they were, they would be finished.

Duncan heard the sound of a thousand arrowheads skidding on hardened sand, just a few feet behind him, and he took a deep breath. Dropping the shields had given him the few extra feet he'd needed.

Duncan saw the great cliffs looming ahead of him, but a hundred yards away now, and he scanned the wall of rock, searching for signs of the small hidden passageways he knew were there. He searched frantically, his heart pounding, knowing that finding these passages would be their only hope of making it back. They had no time to make a mistake: if they pursued a false indent in the rock, they would not have time to search again. If they chose a passageway that was sealed up inside the mountain, they would lose their only chance.

Duncan's heart soared as he spotted a hidden opening in the rock, one just large enough to accommodate him and his men, single file, on horseback—though they would have to duck. The passage led into blackness, and Duncan could only hope it had not collapsed, or would not lead to a dead end. The lives of all his men depended on him now.

Duncan lowered his head. His decision was made.

"SINGLE FILE! CHARGE!" he cried.

Duncan heard his men fall in behind him as he lowered his head and made for the tiny opening in the cliff. He lay with his stomach entirely flat on his horse, the only way of clearing it, and as the rock loomed, he prayed for dear life. He cared not for his own life, but for those of his men.

Please god, he prayed. *Let this work. Give us one chance to battle the Pandesians face to face, man to man. Do not let us die here, in this rock.*

A moment later, Duncan braced himself as he tore into the tiny passageway.

All was blackness. Duncan's heart pounded in his throat as he found himself immersed in a tunnel so cramped that, if he did not duck down, his head would scrape the ceiling. He felt this was an advantage, as he knew it would confuse and slow the Pandesians behind him, too.

Behind him, he heard all his men charging on his heels. He knew that if this tunnel led to a dead end, they would all stampede and crush each other to death. His throat went dry, his palms sweaty, as he clutched the reins and prayed for daylight.

Duncan galloped, his heart pounding, riding faster and faster, twisting and turning, feeling his way in the dark. With every bend he hoped and prayed he would see the way out, a burst of sunlight. Yet still, it did not come.

Finally, as he rounded a sharp bend, his arms and shoulders scraping against the wall, Duncan looked up ahead and his heart burst with joy to see his first glimpse of light. It was a bright shaft of sunlight, an opening up ahead, and it grew brighter with each step. He had never been so eager in his life to embrace it.

A few moments later Duncan fund himself bursting out of the tunnel, into the other side of the cliffs, back to the northern side of the Gulch. He was overjoyed to see dozens of his men eagerly awaiting him, to hear their shouts of triumph, to be reunited with them all. He kept riding, and behind him, all his men burst through, too, one at a time. He could hear their shouts of joy and relief as he did.

When his last man rode through, Duncan immediately dismounted and rushed for the opening. He knew the Pandesians would be on their heels, and there was little time. He was joined by his men as he put his shoulder into a boulder, and they shoved the huge rock with all they had. Duncan, sweating, grunting with the other men, finally managed to roll the ton of rock, sealing off the tunnel's opening.

As soon as it fell into place, there came a boom from the other side; it was the sound, Duncan knew, of the first Pandesian riding into it. Duncan listened as dozens more came, all the Pandesians who had followed them inside, trampling each other to death.

The passageway sealed, Duncan took his first deep breath. He and his men had done it. They had lured the Pandesians to the other side and had returned. His men let out a great cheer as they all realized, and reunited with the men, they all embraced them.

Duncan, as thrilled as he was, knew they had little time. The Pandesians were surely turning back even now, trying to make it back through the Gulch. They had but minutes to seal it off completely before all they had accomplished was undone.

Duncan immediately jumped into action, ignoring the pain and leading his men as he climbed the ropes alongside the cliffs. Each step took them higher and higher, until they finally reached the very heights of the Gulch.

They all stood on the broad plateau up top, Duncan knocked off balance by the driving gale up here, coming off the ocean on the far side of the Gulch. The view from up here was commanding. He looked out and saw the limitless ocean, then he looked down and saw, to the South, Ra's one hundred thousand men, all slowly turning around and heading back for the Gulch. Duncan could see Ra and his golden chariot from here, in the center of it all, gleaming, racing back and realizing finally he had been duped. Duncan saw the gaping passageway of the Gulch, still wide open, and he knew that if he didn't seal it, within minutes the Pandesian army would return to this side of Escalon.

"POSITIONS!" Duncan yelled.

His men all lined up at the edge of the cliff, awaiting his command, and he finally raised one fist and gave the signal. Duncan rushed forward and put his shoulder into the first of the dozens of huge boulders lined up along the cliff's edge, while all around him his men did the same.

Duncan pushed the first huge boulder off the edge, and beside him, dozens more rained down. There followed a tremendous crashing noise, as a great avalanche was set in motion below.

Duncan leaned over the edge and watched. Explosion followed explosion, so strong that the ground shook even up here. The narrow pass of the Devil's Gulch became clogged, one at a time, with massive boulders, all smashing down in a huge cloud of dust and rock. One at a time, higher and higher, they landed atop each other, filling up the Gulch. Soon, it was a wall of rock from here to the sea.

Impassable.

The first vanguard of the Pandesian army, riding too fast to slow down, charged right into the wall of rock. They smashed into it, and with the Gulch sealed up and nowhere to go, they were stampeded from behind, and crushed to death in a great pile of men and horses.

Duncan's men, all watching, let out a great cheer all around him. They had finally sealed the gulch, had finally shut out the great invader.

Duncan felt elated, a great sense of joy. Yet as he looked down, something troubled him. He spotted a small opening in the wall of rock, a spot where one of the boulders had gotten lodged too high above the other. It allowed for a ten-foot tunnel through which Pandesians could slip through the Gulch. Indeed, he saw the Pandesians spot it, too, and make for it. Duncan knew there was no time: the Gulch had to be sealed off completely or else the entire dam would break.

As Duncan studied it, he could tell there was no way to fix it not from up here, not with the rock lodged the way it was. The only way, he knew, was to get down there himself and do it by hand.

Duncan's heart pounded as he felt a sudden thrill. It was the thrill of destiny. The thrill of battle. The thrill of the bold. He knew what he had to do, and he knew there would be no way out. It would mean his death—and yet also the salvation of his nation.

"Commander. Lead these men in my absence," Duncan commanded.

Volen, standing beside him, stared back at Duncan with fear, realizing what he intended to do. He gripped his arm.

"You must not go. It will mean your death."

Duncan could see his old friend had read his mind. And Duncan knew he was right. There would be no way back.

"If I do not," Duncan replied, "then what am I? What is Escalon?"

Duncan gently shook Volen's hand off, turned to the cliffs, and immediately climbed down the rock face, his palms sweaty, his heart pounding in his chest, knowing this would be his final descent.

As he climbed down, faster and faster, scraping elbows and knees and not caring, Duncan felt a great sense of destiny, of clarity, rise up within him. His vision became blurry as he thought of nothing else but that rock below, of sealing off the Gulch for good. Of saving his people. This was what he had been born to do. He was not afraid. He was only grateful that he had been given such a moment, such an opportunity, to die with honor.

Suddenly, Duncan spotted motion out of the corner of his eye and he turned, halfway down the cliff, to see, with horror, a massive boulder sailing through the air. He realized, too late, that the Pandesians were firing catapults, the boulders sailing like weapons toward his men, high up on the plateau, unsuspecting.

There came an awful crash high above as the cliffs shook—and Duncan's heart dropped to hear his men, high above, shrieking. Several of them suddenly fell right past him, their bodies whooshing down toward the Gulch. He looked down and, heart breaking, watched them land, dead.

Duncan saw more catapults being rolled forward, and he did not hesitate. He climbed all the way down the cliffs, right into the center of the gulch. He jumped down to the ground and found, waiting for him, a dozen Pandesian soldiers. Before he could reach the lodged boulder, he had to fight his way past these men.

Rising above his pain, Duncan took a deep breath and threw himself into battle, raising his sword, slashing a charging soldier across the chest, then sidestepping, ducking a blow, and stabbing another in the gut. Duncan ducked a swing of a mace, then spun, raising his sword and blocking a soldier's halberd. He stepped up and elbowed him in the nose, dropping him to the ground.

Duncan fought like a man possessed, cutting through these soldiers like a whirlwind, needing to fight his way across the Gulch. He was completely immersed in the enemy, and he fought like it. He fought like a man who knew he was going to die and had nothing to lose. It brought back the old days, the days when he was but a soldier, free to be reckless, to fight as he wished.

By the time he was done, Duncan, in a mad blur, had felled a dozen soldiers single-handedly. He managed to fight his way all the way to the lodged boulder, then leapt up onto it and climbed his way to the top. A soldier lunged for his leg, and he turned and raised his boot and kicked him in the face right before the soldier could slash it.

Duncan reached down, grabbed a long spear from the hand of a dead Pandesian soldier, raised it high, and plunged it into the crack beside the rock, wedging it deeper and deeper, groaning, with all his might. If he could just pry it enough, this boulder would collapse, would plug the hole and seal the Gulch. He cried out to the heavens, his face turning red from effort, every vein in his body about to pop. It moved, but would not roll.

Suddenly, Duncan heard a commotion and he turned to see another catapult rolled forward, aimed right for him. He watched the soldiers raise their swords, preparing to hack the rope, and he knew it was too late. He had nowhere to run, no way to escape the missile that would come his way.

The Pandesians, after all, would kill him.

CHAPTER TWENTY TWO

Aidan sprinted through the tunnel, Motley running and heaving before him, Cassandra and White behind him, all running single file in the tight confines beneath the Devil's Gulch. As Motley ran, struggling, heaving great gasps of air, Aidan knew that if they didn't reach their destination soon, Motley wouldn't make it. He had drunk one too many pints of ale in his lifetime, and he was in no shape for this.

"There!" Motley finally gasped. "Up ahead!"

Aidan shielded his eyes as harsh desert sunlight shone through—and then, there was chaos.

They all burst out of the tunnel, and the world was filled with the deafening noise of a hundred thousand soldiers, the largest gathering of warriors Aidan had ever seen, all thundering by. The Pandesian army raced by but feet in front of him, and Aidan and the others immediately retreated into the shadows, against the rock. Aidan's heart pounded, praying they were undetected, yet he soon realized they had nothing to fear; it was such chaos before him that not a soul noticed. It was like a river of humanity gushing by.

Of course, no one would be looking for them anyway, here, on the other side of the Devil's Gulch, cut off from the rest of Escalon. Aidan was beginning to realize just how reckless and foolhardy this plan was, yet he did not care. He could not let his father come here alone, and he would do anything to help his father's cause.

As Aidan watched them rumble by, like an endless herd of buffalo, he stood against the wall, choking on the cloud of dust, and saw Motley watching them carefully, as if looking for something.

"There!" Motley finally called out, pointing.

Aidan followed his gaze to see a group of Pandesian soldiers stumbling, falling over each as they were stampeded by the hordes behind them. They rolled to the ground, stomped to death by men and then by horses, no one noticing them in the great chaos. Finally, their bodies bounced out of the way of the rest of the army.

Motley turned to Aidan and gave him a knowing look.

"The cruelty of the Pandesian army," he said. "That is the difference between us and them. We look after our own, while they desert them if they fall. With a million men passing through this tiny gulch, some were bound to fall. It is the way of life, my friend. And one man's loss can be another's opportunity."

Motley looked down.

"Can your dog help us?" he asked.

Aidan, realizing what Motley was after, looked down at White, stroking his head.

"Those three soldiers," Aidan instructed White. "Drag them here!"

White was bounding off before Aidan could even finish his words. White bit the first by the shirt and dragged him back to Aidan, then bounded off and dragged the other two, one at a time, all into the safety of the recesses of the cliffs. Aidan stroked his head proudly, as White licked his hand.

Motley, Aidan, and Cassandra quickly stripped the dead soldiers of their armor. Motley undressed, and as he took off his shirt, his big belly was hanging out in the glaring sun, slick with sweat. He squeezed into the largest soldier's shirt and chainmail; it barely fit, but with a great effort he made it work. Aidan and Cassandra stripped the armor off the smaller soldiers, one a boy hardly older than Aidan, the other an older, frail man, who was short; both of their armor fit, although it was a bit large on them both. As Aidan donned the helmet, the face visor kept slipping down.

He looked over at Cassandra and smiled.

"You look like a man," he said to her.

She smiled back before closing her visor.

"And you, a Pandesian boy," she retorted. "In too-large armor."

Aidan turned and looked at Motley and was startled to find him fully dressed in Pandesian armor, looking like a Pandesian soldier. For a moment Aidan, forgetting, gasped in fear.

"Convincing," Aidan said.

"Let's go," Motley said.

"Where now?" Aidan asked, running beside Motley, trying to catch up as he bounded off away from the safety of the cliffs and right into the thick of the Pandesian army.

"To see," Motley replied, "what damage we can do."

Aidan felt a rush of adrenaline as he found himself in the midst of the chaos and confusion of the Pandesian army, running beside Motley, Cassandra, and White right into the eye of the storm. As they ran, suddenly the tide of soldiers stopped, and the Pandesian army turned back the other way. Aidan, confused, joined them.

"What is happening?" he called out to Motley. "Why are they turning back around for the Gulch?"

"Your father," Motley called back. "He has circled back. They are sealing off the Gulch. His plan is working!"

Aidan felt a swell of pride for his father as he turned and ran with the army, all the Pandesians now realizing they had been duped by his father. Aidan looked up to the cliffs, and sure enough, he spotted his father. There he was, Duncan and all his brave men, risking their lives as they shoved down huge boulders. There came one crash after the next, and Aidan was overjoyed to see the Gulch sealed for good. His father had outsmarted them all.

Aidan heard the cheering of his father's men, their jubilant horns booming throughout the cliffs, and he felt a rush of victory. He saw his father push the final boulder over, and he knew they had done it.

Yet there suddenly came the awful sound of Pandesian horns, one after the next. He watched as the Pandesian army fell into organized lines as they turned back for the gulch. Aidan could see that the Pandesians had found a small opening, and under their commander's whips, they were now all marching for it. Within moments, Aidan realized with dread, they would break through and retake the north.

Worse, there came a sudden sharp creaking and groaning noise, and Aidan turned and was shocked to see a long catapult being rolled forward, holding a massive boulder.

"FIRE!" a commander yelled.

The rope was cut, and the catapults snapped, shooting its boulder high into the air. Aidan watched with dread as it smashed into the cliffs and sent several of his father's men shrieking down to their deaths.

The catapults were quickly reloaded, more boulders rolled forward and mounted on them, and their great ropes yanked back.

Aidan suddenly caught motion out of the corner of his eye, and he turned, startled, to see his father was climbing down the cliffs, alone, into the Gulch, into the heart of the enemy. Aidan realized he was trying to pry loose the wedged boulder and seal off the Gulch for good. Aidan's heart leapt with pride at his father's courage—yet also fear for his safety. He did not see how his father could survive this.

"FATHER!" Aidan cried out, not even thinking.

Motley turned and gave him a warning look.

"Are you mad!?" he hissed, looking about at the enemy. Aidan looked, too, and realized that luckily no one had heard his cry in the commotion.

Aidan knew he had to help him. If he did not do something immediately, his father would surely die here, crushed to death by the sailing boulders.

The next boulder in place, the Pandesian commander shouted orders, and Aidan could see the group of soldiers positioning the catapult, aiming it right for his father.

"NO!" Aidan shrieked.

He could not let it happen. Without thinking, he charged for the catapult.

White ran by his side, and as they reached the catapult, White leapt up and sank his fangs into the lead Pandesian soldier's throat, just before he could slice the rope. Aidan, meanwhile, raised a salvaged spear and let out a fierce battle cry as he rushed into the heart of the enemy, exposing himself, he knew, to death. He did not care. His father's life was at stake, and that was all that mattered.

Aidan jammed the spear into the wooden spokes of the catapult's wheel. A moment later, another soldier stepped forward and hacked the great rope.

A rush of air flew past, and Aidan braced himself as the catapult snapped beside him, the spear jamming its spokes. It made a great snapping noise, and Aidan was thrilled to see the catapult snapping in two. His sabotage had worked.

The boulder, as a result, fell short, and instead of killing his father, it smashed into a crowd of Pandesian soldiers, killing dozens of them on the spot.

Mass chaos broke out, and slowly, Aidan saw a group of Pandesian soldiers turn and spot him.

"TRAITOR!" one cried, pointing to Aidan.

"RUN!" Motley cried. "NOW!"

Aidan wanted to stop, to stay there and fight, to do all he could to help his father. After all, he had just managed to save his life, and to kill dozens of Pandesians at the same time. Yet Motley yanked him away, back through the thick crowd of soldiers, and Aidan knew he had no other choice. He was being swarmed, and he could not make a stand against thousands; if they were to have any chance of survival, now was the time to flee.

"MY FATHER!" Aidan cried, resisting.

"You've done all you can do!" Motley cried back. "You've saved his life. He's on his own now."

Aidan found himself yanked back into the cave, joined by Motley, Cassandra, and White, all of them back in the blackness, racing back, once again, for the right side of the Gulch—and to be reunited, Aidan prayed, with his father once again.

Do not die, Father, he prayed silently. *Do not die.*

CHAPTER TWENTY THREE

Duncan braced himself as the boulder flew through the air, cringing, expecting to be crushed. Yet he watched, stunned, as its course was altered. Something had happened at the catapult, almost as if someone had sabotaged it behind enemy lines—and the boulder, instead of crushing him, of ending any chance of sealing the Gulch, fell short. Duncan looked down and watched as it crushed dozens of Pandesians, stopping their advance toward him.

It was a miracle. And the second chance he needed to seal the Gulch for good and save Escalon.

Duncan went back to prying the lodged boulder, straining all his muscles as he pushed the long spear with all his might.

Please, God, he prayed, *give me the strength. I do not ask for life. I ask only to die in victory. To save my people.*

Finally, with a great whooshing noise, the massive boulder, twenty feet in diameter, gave. It rolled, wedged free, and fell toward the ground. With a huge crash and a cloud of dust, it sealed off the Devil's Gulch for good.

Duncan felt a wave of relief unlike any he'd ever had. Finally, his homeland was secure.

The move, though, as Duncan knew it would, left him standing there, alone amidst the enemy, exposed. He turned and looked out and as he saw the flood of Pandesians charging below, he saw a gleaming in the sunlight and saw none other than the Great and Holy Ra himself leading the way, charging right for Duncan. He rode in his chariot, his long golden spear extended before him, and before Duncan could react, Ra hurled it.

In a blur of motion, Duncan watched the spear sail through the air. But it all happened too fast for him to react.

A moment later, Duncan felt blinding pain, pain as he had never felt. It was the pain of a spear entering his chest, coming out the other side. A pain of finality. A pain from which, he knew at once, he would not recover.

Duncan looked up and met Ra's eyes, and his final feeling, curiously, was one of comfort. He had died, at least, by the hand of his enemy, in the midst of his enemy, sealing off the Gulch, saving his nation, ridding Escalon of the plague of Pandesia forever.

His death, and his life, was a victory.

CHAPTER TWENTY FOUR

Kyra raced through the air on Theon's back, gripping his scales as they flew south, driven by a sense of urgency. Her father awaited her, and she could sense his life hung in the balance. With her heightened powers, Kyra was able to sense things more strongly now, and she felt his danger as if it were her own, as if he were right there beside her.

Gripping the Staff of Truth, Kyra was beginning to see things, her vision becoming more clear. She saw her father surrounded by a great and dangerous army; she saw him facing off with Ra; she saw a gulch, boulders, men falling and dying. She saw an epic battle being waged, one in which the entire fate of Escalon hung in the balance. She leaned down and urged Theon on, the clouds whipping her face. She only prayed it was not too late.

All these months spent training with Alva, meeting her mother, flying to Marda, retrieving the staff—it had all been for this, this moment in time, to fight by her father's side. Finally, her destiny was becoming clear. The prophecy, she realized, had perhaps been right all along.

As she dwelled on her father, she could not help but have a sinking premonition that she was already too late. She saw him surrounded, evil forces closing in, and her heart pounded in dismay. If she had just finished her training a bit sooner, had just left Marda a bit sooner, perhaps she would be fighting by his side now.

"Faster, Theon!" she urged.

Theon obliged and Kyra gripped his scales as the two flew so fast she could barely catch her breath, her homeland racing by in a blur below.

Finally, the terrain changed, and as Kyra looked down, she gasped. There, below, was what appeared to be the entire expanse of the Pandesian army, covering her beloved homeland like a nation of ants. She was even more startled to see that they were now on the southern side of the Devil's Gulch and racing north, trying to reenter Escalon. She realized at once that an epic battle was being waged in the Gulch, between the cliffs and the sea, the waves crashing into the rocks on one side, the towering cliffs bordering the men on the other. It was a battle that had the very fate of Escalon at stake.

Kyra watched catapults hurling boulders through the air, smashing into the cliffs; she saw her father's men falling and dying; she saw Pandesian soldiers swarming below, ramming the rock, trying to break through.

"LOWER, THEON!"

As Theon descended, Kyra spotted something amidst the mayhem that made her heart stop. There, standing atop a huge boulder in the center of the Gulch, facing off against the Pandesian army alone, stood her father. There he stood, so proud, making a stand against an army. She watched as he pried loose a great boulder, saw it fall in a cloud of dust to seal the Gulch for good. She had never been more proud of him than at that moment.

And then Kyra watched, horror-struck, as Ra rushed forward on his golden chariot, raised a golden spear, and hurled it into her father's chest.

She felt her entire life collapse inside her as she watched it kill him.

"NO!" she cried.

Theon dove, needing no urging, sensing what she wanted—and he opened his great mouth and roared.

Fire came pouring down. It spread out in waves on the southern side of the Gulch, and hundreds of Pandesians shrieked, flailing, instantly aflame.

Kyra watched as Ra ducked down beneath his golden chariot, taking cover with his men, using them and their armor as shields. His men fled, burned alive, in every direction, unable to escape Theon's wrath, while Ra huddled beneath the chariot, which melted all around him.

As Theon dove low, roaring in fury, the flames rolled, engulfing all the soldiers approaching the Gulch, pushing back the entire Pandesian army. The Pandesian soldiers, realizing, finally turned and fled, away from the Gulch, as Kyra and Theon drove them back.

Kyra pursued them, vengeance burning in her blood. She felt the Staff of Truth summoning her, and she felt a burning urge to use it. She brought it down fiercely, with a great battle cry.

A clap like thunder emanated from it, and a shockwave spread below. It spread through the ranks and destroyed thousands of men of the Pandesian army within moments. She struck again and again, decimating all she saw before her, unleashing an unstoppable wave of fury and destruction. She pushed the Pandesians further and further south, far away from the Gulch, forcing them to turn and flee all the way back for their homeland.

Kyra finally circled around. She could finish off the army some other time. What was most pressing was her father, who lay there in the Gulch, flat on his back. Perhaps there was still time to save him.

"DOWN, THEON!" she urged.

Theon dove down and landed beside her father, atop a wide, flat boulder in the center of the Gulch. Kyra dismounted and rushed to her father's side.

She knelt beside him, wracked with sobs as she picked him up in her arms. His eyes were closed, his breathing shallow. He was alive—barely.

"Father!" she wept, tears gushing down her cheeks, unable to contain her grief.

She picked him up in her arms, laid him on Theon's back, then climbed up and held him. They took off, flying back to the northern side of the Gulch, to the safety of his men. If there was any chance of saving him, this was the only way.

*

Kyra knelt at her father's side, surrounded by hundreds of his men, all crowding in close, all looking down at Duncan on his deathbed. He was very weak, his eyes barely open, as he lay on the rock, safe amongst his men, on this side of the Gulch. The free side.

In the distance Kyra could hear the Pandesian army, still smarting from their defeat, from the closing of the Gulch. It sounded like they were rallying, preparing for another attack, to try to find a way around the Gulch—or through it. Perhaps. But for now at least, for the first time since this nightmare had begun, Escalon was safe.

And yet, Kyra did not feel safe. She did not feel relieved. Instead, she felt a deep, overwhelming sadness. She knelt there, looking down at her father, watching his life force ebb away, and it pained her to no end. What she thought would never happen was happening. Her father, the greatest, strongest man she had ever known, was dying. All the healers had said his time had come.

Her eyes welled with tears as she looked down, cradling his head in her hands. If only she'd arrived sooner, she thought. Even a few minutes. If only she had broken free from Marda sooner. If only there had been anything she could have done to save his life. She felt as if she had let him down.

She wiped away her tears and willed her father not to die.

"Father," she said, her voice barely above a whisper, "I have failed you."

She waited in the interminable silence. Finally, Duncan reached out and grabbed her wrist, holding it firmly. He smiled weakly, his eyes barely open.

94

"Kyra," he said. His voice sounded so muted, so distant, not like the father she had loved and known, had looked up to her entire life.

She looked down, listening.

"I want you to know something," he added.

She leaned closer, struggling to hear his voice.

"You have made me proud. Prouder than I could have ever hoped to be as a father. Prouder than my sons." He paused, trying to speak. "More importantly, I want you to know how much I love you."

Kyra could not hold back her tears as her father struggled to breathe, to speak.

"*You*, Kyra," he finally added. "You, of all my children, are the one. Tell your mother…"

His voice trailed off, and Kyra's heart pounded with curiosity and regret, as she felt all her emotions overwhelming her. He could not die. Not now. She *willed* for him not to die.

"What, Father?" she cried. "Tell her what? What should I tell my mother? Who is my mother? Who am I?"

Duncan laid his head back down, closed his eyes, and uttered his final words.

"Tell her…" he concluded, "…I am sorry."

With that, Duncan's eyes closed.

Dead.

Kyra let out a wail of grief. She leaned back and looked to the skies, cursing this day. Life was too cruel. Was there not already enough death in the world to spare this one man?

Kyra suddenly felt utterly alone, more alone than she had ever felt in the universe. She felt like an orphan. It didn't seem natural not to have a parent. It didn't seem fair. How could her father be taken away from her, especially now, after such a victory? On the verge of achieving complete freedom? On the verge of achieving everything he had ever hoped and dreamed of, their entire lives?

Kyra wailed with grief as she leaned over him, hugging his dead body, crying out again and again.

"No, Father, no!"

She wanted to bring him back. To hug him. To tell him how much she loved him. She had imagined celebrating with him, had imagined him always being there to watch her become a great warrior, to see how proud of her he would be. To meet her own children one day. What did she have to live for with her father dead? Whose approval did she have left to win?

Kyra knew at that moment that a part of her had died with him—and that she would never, ever, be the same again.

CHAPTER TWENTY FIVE

Merk and Lorna navigated the ship deeper into the Bay of Ur, the black skies lit eerily by the red twinkling stars and by the glow of Pandesian ships aflame. As they sailed their hull bumped against the endless cadavers of Pandesian soldiers floating in the waters, a soft yet eerie sound. Lorna's mist still hung in the air, but it was beginning to burn off, and slowly, they were losing their cover. Their time was scarce now.

Merk looked over at Lorna and saw her exhaustion, could see from her eyes the toll it had taken on her. With each passing moment their ship would become more visible, and already Merk could hear the Pandesian horns, the shouts of soldiers preparing to rally and fight back.

"Where do we sail, my lady?" Merk asked, feeling an increasing sense of panic. With each passing moment, with each body they passed, they were sailing deeper into the heart of the enemy. They had managed to commandeer a ship—yet they were still surrounded, and vastly outnumbered. It was only a matter of time until the other Pandesian ships discovered that they were the enemy.

Lorna looked out and studied the waters calmly, expressionless, clearly seeing into worlds that Merk would never understand. There followed a long silence in which there came nothing but the gentle splashing of water—and cadavers—against the hull.

Finally, she raised a finger and pointed.

"There."

Merk struggled to follow her gaze, peering into the night and mist until finally he spotted something. It was another ship, and his heart leapt with joy to see it was being sailed by one of theirs. At the helm he recognized Duncan's commander, Seavig, the ship filled with his men. Merk watched as Seavig sailed right for a Pandesian ship, one of the few not aflame, and let out a great battle cry. Without warning, his men leapt from one ship to the other, drawing swords and charging.

Shouts and clangs rang out as they fought man to man, and Merk realized with a jolt that Seavig was trying to take another ship. Merk marveled at their courage, at their recklessness in thinking they could defeat this entire Pandesian fleet. He watched dozens of Pandesians fall, and yet saw many of Seavig's men fall, too. More horns sounded, and Pandesian ships rallied, turning for Seavig's ship. Merk watched, wide-eyed, as in the distance the

Pandesians raised cannons. He knew that if he did not do something quick, Seavig and his men would be wiped out for good.

Merk rushed to the cannon on his own ship, pushed it with all his might, and aimed it for the distant Pandesian ship. He lit a torch and raised it, and looked to Lorna.

"This will give away our position," he said grimly. "If I do this, we will be surrounded."

She nodded back her approval.

He lowered the flame to the wick, and a moment later there came a tremendous boom, the force of it knocking him back.

The cannonball flew through the air and smashed into the hull of the Pandesian ship before it could fire on Seavig. Merk watched it buckle and sink, and was elated to see he had saved Seavig's men.

Merk heard commotion behind them, and he turned to see, as the last of the mist rose, Pandesian ships had spotted him. They began to close in. He knew that within moments they would be surrounded.

Merk heard a shout of triumph, and he turned to see Seavig's men had taken the other ship, throwing the last dead Pandesian overboard. There followed a loud rattling, and he then watched as Seavig and his men threw long spiked chains overboard. Finally, as they set sail, Merk realized what their strategy was. Seavig had commandeered the larger ship for its huge supply of chains. As they sailed, his men threw them overboard and held on tight, dragging them along the water.

Merk looked out and saw that they were sailing for the far end of the harbor, and he realized right away what they were doing: they were trying to seal it off. They were goading the entire Pandesian fleet to follow them into the harbor, hoping to secure the chains first and destroy their hulls. It was a brilliant move. If they succeeded, they would sink half the fleet outside the harbor and cut off the other half, leaving them trapped inside the harbor.

Merk's heart raced as he watched Seavig make good progress, sailing quickly, the air filled with rattling as his men lowered chain link after link.

Horns sounded again and again, and Merk turned to see more Pandesian ships rallying, spotting Seavig. They were closing in, and Merk knew that in a hundred yards or so they would destroy Seavig. They were not going to make it.

At the same time, Merk turned and realized that the other ships that had spotted him and Lorna were getting closer.

Merk shoved the cannon with all his might, raised a heavy cannonball, and lit the torch. It fired with a boom, sending him backwards, and he watched with satisfaction as it took out the ship trailing them, right before they could fire themselves.

More ships closed in, and as Merk looked down at the deck, he was aghast to see there were no more cannonballs.

He turned to Lorna, knowing something had to be done. He felt the turning point had come.

"I have to stop them," he said.

She looked at him, concern in her eyes.

"And how shall you?" she asked.

He scanned the waters desperately, and an idea came to him.

"I must board one of the Pandesian ships," he said. "From there, I can fire on the others. I can distract them long enough for Seavig to chain the harbor, to win the battle."

She nodded back in admiration.

"You know that once you fire, you will be surrounded. You will die."

He looked back at her, thinking the same thing, knowing it was true.

"I do," he replied solemnly.

Merk sighed.

"All my life, I've done harm to others," he said. "I regret it with all that I am. I yearn for redemption. I yearn to do right for something bigger than myself. I have found that chance. If I stop that fleet, Seavig will seal off the harbor. Ur will be free. Escalon can be free once again. What is more important?"

He took a step closer.

"This is my chance, Lorna. My chance to become the man I had always wished I had been."

She looked back at him, her eyes shining, intense.

"I care for Escalon as much as you," she said. "But I care for you, too. I don't want to see you die."

Merk felt overwhelmed, realizing for the first time that Lorna actually cared for him. And that meant more to him than he could say. His resolve deepened.

Without a word, he stepped forward and kissed her.

It was a kiss that restored his soul. He expected her to back away, and he was stunned that she did not.

Finally, they parted, gently.

"I love you," he said.

He did not wait for a reply. With those words, Merk turned, leapt off the edge of the ship, and dove headlong down into the freezing waters of the harbor of Ur.

"Merk!" he heard her call out behind him.

A moment later Merk found himself immersed in the freezing waters, and as he did, his body in shock, he forced himself to stay under, not wanting to be detected. He swam and swam underwater, kicking, using his arms, until finally he could hold his breath no longer and surfaced far away, near the hulls of the Pandesian ships. He stealthily reached up, grabbed the rope dangling down from one of them, and pulled himself up, dripping wet, one foot at a time. Muscles aching, he pulled as quietly as he could as he inched his way up the hull, praying he was not detected.

Finally, Merk stealthily climbed over the rail and set foot on the Pandesian deck. He looked out and saw hundreds of soldiers on board, and his apprehension deepened. Yet it was too late now.

Merk braced himself and took off at a sprint. He extracted his dagger, ran up to the soldier he saw manning the cannon, and as he turned, Merk sliced his throat. He caught him before he hit the ground, putting him down gently so as not to alert the others.

Merk then grabbed the torch, and with all his might kicked the heavy cannon into position, knowing he had but one chance at this.

"Hey!" a voice called out behind him.

He glanced back to see the Pandesians charging.

Merk lit the cannon, leaving himself exposed and no longer caring. He was no longer concerned for himself; he cared only for saving Seavig and his men.

Merk lowered the torch, lit the cannon, and a great sparking filled the air. Out of the corner of his eye he saw soldiers rushing him from all sides, and he prayed only that the cannon caught fire before they could reach him.

"STOP!" one cried.

BOOM!

The cannon fired a second before the men reached him, knocking them all back several feet. Merk watched with relief as the cannonball soared exactly where he wanted it to: through the hulls of all the Pandesian ships floating alongside this one. It tore through one after another, shattering a half dozen of them at once.

Cries and chaos filled the air, as one Pandesian ship after another sank.

As the soldiers were collecting themselves, Merk knew he had but a moment left. He rolled, placed one more cannonball, grabbed the torch and lit the other cannon, as he turned it with all his might.

A Pandesian soldier tackled him, sending him down to the ground, while another Pandesian soldier tried desperately to stop the cannon, screaming as he tried to put it out.

But it was too late.

BOOM!

The cannon was positioned straight down, and the cannonball smashed through its own ship, shattering it to pieces. Merk felt the ship buckle and splinter beneath him.

In the chaos of the wildly rocking ship, Merk looked up to see a soldier charging, a long spear coming right at him. Before he could sit up, he felt unbearable pain as the soldier stabbed him right through the heart.

Merk gasped, unable to breathe. He felt the awful shock of his life departing him. On his back, he looked up to the night sky, filled with red stars, and he felt, for the first time in his life, a sense of peace. Redemption had found him. Even in death.

CHAPTER TWENTY SIX

Kyle, in the thick of the rubble of the Tower of Ur, fought his way through the battlefield of trolls, Leo at his side, swinging his staff, striking them down two, three, four at a time. Kolva, by his side, fought equally ferociously, too, the two of them fighting for each inch as they tried to make their way towards the center of the rubble. They had to reach the secret chamber, the only hope, as Alva had explained, to restore the Flames and ensure victory for Escalon.

Alva's words still rang in Kyle's ears. *Beneath the Tower of Ur lies the secret chamber.* The ramifications of his words were staggering. Could it be true? Kyle wondered. Could it be that the Tower of Ur had never been a decoy after all? That its most precious secret lay not above ground all this time—but below? A secret chamber which controlled the very fate of Escalon?

Kyle swung with his staff and smashed one troll in the face, then spun around and jabbed another in the throat, while Kolva ducked from a halberd swing and smashed a troll across the chest with his staff. The two of them pushed back the trolls as dozens more appeared every moment, bridging Alva's fissure. It was a never-ending stream. They swung mighty halberds; one troll neared and swung broadly for Kyle's head, and Kyle ducked, the blade whistling in the air above him, and realized that if he were but a second later it would have decapitated him. He swung his staff around and cracked the troll in the ribs, breaking them, then brought his staff down on the troll's back, smashing its neck and dropping it. Beside him, Kolva stepped forward and jabbed a troll between the eyes, and the beast dropped to its knees.

Kyle heard a snarl behind him, and he turned, aghast, to see a troll lowering a halberd for his head. Kyle was too late—he had missed this one. And with Kolva and Leo preoccupied, he braced himself for the end.

Suddenly, a vicious snorting noise came as Kyle detected motion out of the corner of his eye. His heart flooded with relief to see Andor appearing, galloping onto the rubble. Before the troll could lower his halberd, Andor threw himself at him, trampling him to death. Andor pinned him down, crushing him, then sank his sharpened teeth into the troll's throat, killing him for good.

Kyle looked back at Kyra's horse in awe of this magnificent creature, his fearlessness, his loyalty.

Kyle fought his way once again for the center, this time, Andor fighting beside him. They had almost reached the center of the rubble, yet every time they dropped one troll, ten more appeared. They were losing momentum.

"Go!" Kolva called out, as he slashed at a troll's chest, sending him flying back through the air. "Make for the center! I'll hold them off!"

Kyle leapt over a halberd swing and cracked two more in the chest.

"If I leave you," he called back, "you won't last long!"

"Then go quickly!" Kolva called back.

Leo lunged and sank his teeth into a troll's chest, Andor trampled several more, and Kolva stepped forward, creating cover for Kyle, distracting the trolls, and Kyle knew this was his chance: he turned and ran for the center of the rubble. He jumped and climbed his way over massive boulders, the debris from the tower's collapse. This ancient place where he had once lived, once so magnificent, its upper levels grazing the sky, was now, it pained Kyle to see, nothing but a mountain of rock.

Kyle finally reached the dead center of where the tower had once stood, and, with Kolva distracting the trolls, he had a monetary lull in the battle. He bent down and clawed at the rock, anxious to find the opening to the lower levels.

It was futile. He could not even budge the massive boulders, his hands chafed from the effort.

Desperate, Kyle raised his staff, closed his eyes, and summoned his ancient power, the power that always coursed through his blood as a Watcher. He used it rarely, yet he knew it was needed for a time like this. He opened his eyes, raised his staff, and brought it straight down. He felt it smashing through rock, and he kept on going until he had created a hole. He shoved his staff side to side, widening it, creating an opening in which to enter.

Kyle looked down at the opening in the earth, felt the cool damp air flowing up at him, and was stunned to realize he was staring into the very foundation of the Tower of Ur. The lower levels, previously hidden beneath the rubble, were now visible to him, a gaping hole in the blackness.

Kyle glanced back and saw Kolva still fighting off the trolls. He knew Kolva's situation was precarious, with more trolls streaming in every moment.

"GO!" Kolva urged. "You are the last hope."

Kyle leapt, jumping down into the earth.

Kyle felt himself falling deeper and deeper into the very depths of blackness, the cool air enveloping him. He finally landed with a painful thump, rolling onto his ribs, feeling as if he had broken them.

Kyle crawled to his hands and knees and gathered his wits about him in the darkness. He had fallen a good twenty feet, landing in a puddle of water on a smooth granite floor. He breathed, slowly coming back to himself.

A cold draft ran over his hands, and water dripped somewhere. High up above he could hear the muffled fighting of the trolls. He marveled that he was back here, in the Tower of Ur, albeit in the sub-levels. All the years he had lived here, no one had been allowed to descend. Kyle had never thought much of it. He had always assumed that the tower's secrets lay in the highest levels, not the lowest.

But now he realized he had, all this time, been wrong. What could he expect to find down here? What had Alva been alluding to?

As he squinted to adjust his eyes, Kyle spotted a small, flickering torchlight in the distance. He saw smooth, ancient corridors of black marble before him, and he felt a vibration within him. He felt a great power, and sensed something momentous lay just around the bend.

Kyle followed the corridors, turning down one after the next, his bootsteps echoing, until finally he reached an arched, stone door, twice as tall as he, framed by flickering torches. It was carved from one slab of marble, engraved with ancient inscriptions, and he ran his finger along the symbols in awe. He hadn't seen the lost languages for centuries. He knew that something momentous must lie beyond that door.

Kyle reached out to the marble knob and tried it. To his dismay, it did not work.

He put his shoulder into it, pushed with all his might, yet it would not budge.

Kyle, determined, felt a great heat rising within him as he closed his eyes, took a deep breath, and summoned his power. He then raised his staff, let out a cry, and smashed the door with all his might. He smashed it again and again and again, blows that would have been powerful enough to knock down a mountain.

Yet to his shock, the stone door still would not budge.

Kyle stood there, sweating, stumped. He recalled the legends of his ancestors, legends he had been told as a boy, and in the back of his mind, he recalled the myth of the sacred chamber. Could this be it? He had never fully understood it at the time, yet now, as he examined this door, it began to make sense to him. He recalled the ancient chanting he had heard as a boy, aimed at summoning the core power of the universe.

Could it be? he wondered.

Kyle set his staff down on the ground, then reached out and touched the door with both palms. A power greater than the staff, he knew, would be needed here.

Closing his eyes, he chanted, softly at first, then with greater volume and conviction. He began to feel an unbearable heat on his palms, as if his hands were really on fire. It was as if he and the door were one.

And a moment later, to his shock, there came a soft click.

Kyle looked down, amazed to see the door had opened. Ancient air, trapped for centuries, slowly released.

He pushed the door open slowly, looked into the chamber, and froze.

He could not believe what lay before him.

CHAPTER TWENTY SEVEN

Kyra slowly lowered the flickering torch to her father's dead body as it lay on the raised funeral pyre, at eye level with her, and as she did, she felt as if she were lowering the torch on herself. Inside, her heart was breaking. She wept quietly, surrounded by his hundreds of warriors, all of them crowding in close, her weeping the only sound in the thick silence, complemented only by the howling of the wind, making the flames ripple. Kyra felt the tears pour down her cheeks, as they had for hours, and she no longer tried to stop them. She felt numb to the world, hollowed out. Seeing her father dead before her, she felt as if all that was best in her had been stolen away.

Kyra knelt there, torch in her shaking hand, and could not bring herself to lower it. She could not bear to touch the funeral pyre, to set her father aflame and send him to the gods. Something inside her just would not allow it.

She was not the only one: beside her stood her brother, Aidan, staring straight ahead, frozen, numb, eyes wide in a vacant stare that was more terrifying than her father's death. It was as if his life had been robbed of him. White sat at his feet, looking equally despondent.

"Don't do it," he said to her slowly, darkly, looking at the torch as if it were a snake.

Her heart broke at his words.

With all eyes on her, Kyra stood there, frozen, numb. She did not think she would be able to do it.

To her relief, Motley stepped forward, breaking the silence, joined by several more actors. A small group of them stood there before her, and she looked up at them, puzzled. She wondered what they were going to do.

They all turned, faced the pyre, held hands, and looked up at the sky. Then one of them leaned back, and to her surprise, began to sing a song.

It was a slow, haunting tune, filling the solemn air. The others joined in, and the chorus gained volume. It was a nostalgic song, a song of her childhood, and the flood of feelings it evoked was too much for Kyra. Images flashed through her mind. She recalled all the times her father had sat with her, close to the fire, reading her stories, reciting legends, tales of the past, teaching her, urging her to be a warrior.

And yet, as they continued to sing, Kyra also slowly felt a sense of resolution. It was a feeling of rebirth. She could not help but feel as if it was her father's soul who wanted her to hear the song, as a reminder of all the times they had spent together, sitting and reading, all those nights that inspired her, that had made her know who she wanted to be.

How much more will this war take from us? she asked her father silently. *How much more will be stripped away? Will anything be left when it is done? Will it all even be worth it?*

She closed her eyes and felt herself speaking to her father, and she never wanted to open them, to return to this world. Sometimes reality, she realized, was more painful than fantasy.

Kyra did not know how much time had passed before she felt a gentle hand on her shoulder. She looked up to find her brother, Aidan, looking down, his eyes red with tears, Cassandra standing beside him, White at their feet. She saw his pain, and it brought her back. She realized others were suffering, too, not just her, and somehow it made her feel less alone. She felt for her little brother; he had lost so much, so quickly, and he was far too young to have to endure this all. He was now the only family she had left.

She felt a strong hand on her other shoulder and she looked up to see Anvin standing on her other side, eyes red. Behind him stood dozens of her father's soldiers, and she saw they were all grieving, too. She realized that they also seemed lost. After all, their commander had been taken away from them. She began to think of others and what they must be going through, and not only of herself.

The song ended, and Kyra took a deep breath, calming her tears, slowly letting it out. She felt the eyes of all the great warriors were now upon her, men who had looked to her father for leadership, men who needed direction now. Somewhere in the distance, as her world came back into focus, there came the distant sounds of war, the sounds of the Pandesian army, somewhere on the other side of the Gulch. She could hear Theon pawing the earth, not far away, stomping the ground impatiently. She was stuck in time, and she knew that time could not be frozen forever. She had to be strong. It was what her father would have wanted of her. It was what, she sensed, he was trying to tell her.

Kyra, seeing the faces of all these proud men about her, slowly began to feel a new resolve arise within her. She felt the spirit of her father, the strength of her father, a great warlord, coursing through her. She felt that her strength was giving her father peace. She felt him smiling down at her, trying to speak to her.

Kyra, he said in her mind, *I will always be with you. Let me go. Release me. Release me, and my spirit will be bigger than it ever was. It will be a part of you, forever.*

Wiping away her final tears, Kyra slowly stood, a cold, steely resolve within her. As she did, she reached out and slowly lowered the torch.

A moment later, to her own shock, the pyre was ablaze.

It rippled in the wind, flames rising higher and higher. All the men around her backed away from the intense heat. But not she. She was used to flame. She rode, after all, on the back of a dragon.

Instead, Kyra inched closer. She wanted to feel the heat. She wanted to feel a bit of pain. She wanted to implant this day on her mind forever. A part of her, indeed, still wished to die with him.

Soon enough, the pyre burned down, all that remained a pile of ashes, of falling embers, where her father's body had once been. She looked down at it, numb. It did not seem possible. Was life that fleeting?

Kyra felt a calloused hand on her wrist, and she looked over to see Anvin. She followed his gaze and saw the torch in her hand, smoking, burnt out for she did not know how long. She had forgotten she was still holding it.

Finally, she opened her hand and released it. It fell to the ground and collapsed in a pile of sparks.

Anvin looked at her, compassion in his eyes.

"Your father loved you more than anything," he said. "More than us. More than battle. You were his soul."

Kyra felt a great wave of grief wash over her. Why could she not have arrived sooner to rescue him?

"His memory lives in you now," he continued. "As does his spirit. Without you, he is truly gone forever. But with you, he can live again."

She pondered his words.

"Do you understand?" he asked. "You are his rightful heir. You are our leader now."

Kyra turned and looked out at all her father's men, and she saw them all staring back somberly, nodding in agreement. Needing her leadership. Needing her father to rise again.

"Your father's goal, our goal, remains unfinished," he continued. "On the other side of those cliffs, a vast Pandesian army rallies. Soon enough, they'll find a way through the Gulch. We must take the fight to them, drive them back once and for all. Will you lead us? Will you become commander of Escalon?"

Kyra heard his words and she could not help but think back to the prophecies, to that fateful night, in the blizzard, when she had first encountered a wounded Theos. She thought of the sorcerer's prophecy, that she would one day rise to be a great warrior, a great leader, even greater than her father. How foolish it had seemed in that moment. Yet ever since then she had also felt an inevitability to the words, and had wondered if, or when, it would come to pass.

Now that the day had arrived, it all felt surreal. As if she were caught up in something bigger than herself. Something always destined to happen.

Slowly, she nodded back.

"My father's soul cries for vengeance," she said, the first words she had uttered since her father's death. Her mouth was still dry; she had not thought she would ever be able to speak again, and her own words surprised her.

She turned and looked out at all the men, feeling how much they needed her now, wanting to give them the inspiration they so deserved.

"And I intend to give it to him," she said, her voice booming, taking on a new strength. It was the strength of a commander.

There arose a cheer amongst the men, and as Kyra raised her staff, they all rallied around her, raising their swords, looking at her with the same love and devotion they had once reserved for her father.

"KYRA!" they cried. "KYRA! KYRA! KYRA!"

CHAPTER TWENTY EIGHT

Seavig sailed with urgency across the harbor of Ur, so close to achieving his goal of sealing off the harbor. Yet even while his men dragged the chains, they also cried out all around him on the ship as they began to fall, killed by Pandesian arrows. Seavig ducked himself as yet another Pandesian arrow landed in the deck beside him. He looked up and saw, amidst the glow of the flames, the sky was filled with them. Too many of his men were not as lucky, gasping in the night as they were punctured by arrowheads all around him. He flinched each time one of his men fell overboard, splashing into the water, food for the sharks. Their time, he knew, was scarce if they were all to survive.

Cannons boomed in the night, and cannonballs splashed in the water all around him, getting too close to his ship. The Pandesian fleet was closing in with each second, and Seavig looked out and saw thousands of ships all now directed toward the harbor, all turning their attention to him. They finally realized that he had been the culprit all along, the one who had commandeered their ship and set hundreds of their other ships aflame. Now, they wanted vengeance.

Seavig knew he had little time left before he and all his men were killed. If he were to succeed in his risky plan, now was his final chance. The dragging of chains, music to his ears, continued as they sailed across the harbor. He glanced back at the stern of the ship and saw the massive spiked chains being dragged, towed underwater in the blackness, just out of sight of the Pandesians. He ran over and helped his men as two of them fell overboard, dragging the chains as they had for hours across the harbor.

He looked ahead, and he saw they were nearly there. Just a hundred more feet, and they would make the far side of the harbor, be able to affix the chain to the stone wall and seal off the harbor for good. If they did, the thousands of ships pursuing him would sail right into their deaths, their hulls cracked to bits on the spiked, submerged chain.

As for the hundreds more Pandesian ships trapped inside the harbor, Seavig had another idea. But first he had to destroy the fleet pursuing him.

"FASTER!" he called out to his men.

A fierce splashing arose as his dozens of men rowed even faster. They heaved on the long oars, the splashing cutting into the night. Seavig had never made his men work so hard, some rowing, some fighting back, firing arrows back into the night, while still more raised shields and blocked for the others. He ran over and helped them row, yet still, too many of his men fell, their cries and shouts piercing the night.

Seavig suddenly winced in pain as an arrow, sailing through the night, found a spot through his shoulder. He slumped down, dropping his oar, seated at the head of his men, and clutched the wound. He gritted his teeth and shrieked as he broke the arrow in half and extracted it, leaving the arrowhead in. Face drenched in sweat, he took a deep breath and forced himself to continue to row, despite the pain. He could feel his men looking at him with surprise and pride, and he knew he had to set an example.

Seavig rowed and rowed, looking to the harbor wall, his arm and shoulder burning, not knowing how much longer he could go on. Finally, to his immense relief, he felt the ship's hull hitting stone. The whole ship shook with the impact, and they came to a sudden stop.

Seavig jumped to his feet, wasting no time.

"THE CHAINS!" he yelled.

The men at the stern grabbed the chain and pulled with all their might as they yanked it across the deck. They formed a line, each man handing off the chain links to the next, as it made its way along the length of the ship.

Seavig rushed to the bow and looked down into the waters below and spotted a huge iron hook affixed to the stone wall of the shore; covered in rust, it had clearly stood there for thousands of years. His ancestors had affixed it there for times like this, times when their harbor was invaded, when their nation was in danger. It had, after all, always been the way of the men of Escalon to prepare for times of war. It was the same in all the major port cities, and in his own city of Esephus, too. Which was why Seavig knew exactly where to look.

Seavig, holding the chain, looked down at the steep drop and knew there was no other choice. Someone had to affix it, and he did not want to leave such a risky job to his men. It was now or never.

Seavig let out a cry as he jumped through the air, holding the chain, and fell twenty feet toward the black harbor below. A moment later he was submerged in the icy waters, losing his breath, still clutching the chain as he kicked his feet, struggling to surface.

Finally, he did, gasping for air, shaking off the shock of the cold, and began to swim as best he could while dragging the heavy chain.

Seavig, gasping with every breath, the wound in his arm bleeding into the water, killing him, finally reached the sea wall. He clawed at the slippery, moss-covered stone and fell back into the water too many times. He reached up again and caught a finger in a crack, jammed his boot in an indent and pulled his way up, still holding the chain, freezing, blood oozing from his wound.

Seavig managed to claw his way up several feet, arms shaking, knowing he was in danger of falling at any moment. He looked up and saw the huge hook above, yet it was feet away. It might as well have been a mile away.

Come on, he willed himself. *Don't give up.*

Seavig reached with the chain high overhead, hands shaking as he tried again and again to slip it over the hook. It was just too high.

Come on.

He thought of Duncan, thought of all the great warriors of Escalon, and he felt a strength rise within him, a primal strength he always knew he had. He groaned as he stretched, and finally, he slipped it over the hook. He yanked on it to make sure it was secure, and just as he did, he fell backwards, into the waters.

Duncan quickly surfaced and looked up. It was a beautiful sight. From here, all the way to the other side of the harbor, the chain stretched, hundreds of feet across, hiding just below the surface. He tested it and it snapped to, taut, spiked, menacing. It would be a thing of death for the thousands of Pandesian ships sure to follow them into the harbor.

Seavig swam to his ship as his men threw down ropes, and grabbed hold as his men pulled him up. He held on tight as his men hauled him up.

Seavig, breathing heavily, landed on deck as his men grabbed him and pulled him over, embracing him.

Now on this side of the harbor, Seavig felt protected, knowing the only way the fleet could reach him was by sailing through that chain. He looked out and was thrilled to see thousands of Pandesian ships following, all rushing to catch up with each other. They were all so tight, moving so fast, so bent on vengeance, that they would be unable to turn around in time. It would be a slaughter.

Yet he knew there was no time to celebrate yet.

"TO THE LOCKS!" he cried.

His men rushed into action, redirecting the ship as they sailed for shore. They sailed as far from the chains as they could—and he braced himself as moments later, the first unsuspecting Pandesian ship sailed right into it.

The sharp sound of cracking wood cut through the air, like lightning. Seavig watched with a feeling of awe and victory as the first Pandesian ship buckled, its soldiers looking around perplexed, wondering what they could possibly be sailing into as they looked overboard. Yet they had no time to figure it out. Within moments, the ship buckled into itself and sank, bow first. Soldiers shrieked as they fell like ants, sliding off the deck and into the waters, immediately dragged down by the currents and their heavy armor.

Dozens more ships followed in their wake, sailing full speed into the chains, all trying to pursue Seavig into the harbor. Their bloodlust got the better of them, and their ships cracked and broke up into the quickly forming graveyard in the sea. The chains held, and Seavig's men let out a cheer as it was clear they were now safe from the main Pandesian fleet, locked out of the harbor.

Soon the water was littered with the wood of thousands of Pandesian ships, debris piled high. Floating amongst these were the corpses of thousands more soldiers, floating on their stomachs, food for the sharks that quickly materialized and snatched them up. The destruction and chaos was intense as the Pandesian fleet was dismantled ship by ship.

Seavig now prepared himself to fight the battle on the other front. He turned and looked back to shore, and he remembered they were not safe yet. There were still hundreds more Pandesian ships here, inside the harbor, on this side of the chain line. They began to rally, to close in on Seavig, and he knew he had to do something quick or die at their hands.

"THE LOCKS!" he cried again.

Seavig steered his ship toward the massive stone levers which he knew would be embedded in the side of Ur's original canals. He had sailed this harbor many times as a boy with his father's fleet, and he knew all the locks' locations, the same locations the locks were placed in Esephus. In times of war, the locks could be used to drain the harbor, to drain the canals, and to spare the city an attack by water. If the locks could be lowered, the seawall could be raised, protecting the harbor, sealing it off from the sea, and draining the city. It was, Seavig knew, the key to final victory.

Their ship finally slammed into the seawall, and Seavig wasted no time. He raced across the deck with his men, and they reached out and threw ropes, securing their ship to the wall. They all crowded in and reached out, desperate to grab hold of the massive stone lever. Seavig led the way, and he reached out and grabbed hold of the ancient lever, as big as he, protruding from the seawall. Several of his men joined in as he pushed down with all he had, all of them groaning from the effort.

Yet it would not budge.

A cannon boomed, a cannonball splashed in the water beside their ship, and Seavig, sweating, turned to see the ships closing in. He knew that their next shot would be accurate. He had no time. If these locks failed, he and his men would surely die here.

"HARDER!" Seavig cried. "Push with all you have!"

Dozens more of his men rushed forward, and as one, they all pushed harder and harder, yanking at the ancient stone lever until their hands turned raw. Seavig thought he might die from the effort.

And then, finally, it happened. To Seavig's joy, the massive lever began to budge. There came the sound of stone scraping stone, as inch by inch, it began to move.

They gained momentum, and there came a great whooshing noise. Seavig looked over and was amazed as he watched the ancient seawall rising up through the waters, higher and higher, slowly sealing off the harbor. They groaned from the effort as they slowly finished securing the lock and the seawall rose all the way, blocking off the harbor of Ur from the rest of the sea.

At the same time, huge drainage pipes were opened alongside the canals, and the sound of gushing water filled the air. The waters that had flooded the city of Ur began to recede as quickly as they had flooded it. It drained so quickly that Seavig felt his ship rocking beneath him, and he looked down to see his boat sinking as the water level dropped, lower and lower.

Seavig felt his stomach dropping as they sank a hundred feet within a minute. As they did, the Pandesian ships in the harbor sank with them. Slowly, all the ancient buildings of the city of Ur began to appear again, as if rising from the grave. Seavig's heart was lifted as, foot by foot, the city rose again.

Seavig's ship was soon sitting on dry land, on the seabed, in a dry harbor. He looked out and saw the hundreds of Pandesian ships on dry ground now, too. They all looked down, baffled, clearly not expecting this. Their ships' hulls, tapered at the bottom, began to sway as they hit the mud, then started to topple.

Moments later, the first ship keeled over, falling flat on its side.

Thousands of Pandesian soldiers, shrieking, fell fifty feet from their ships, down to the muddy ground, some dying on impact. The ones who survived scurried to regain their footing, then drew swords and rushed to attack Seavig's men.

Seavig would not wait for them.

"Men of Escalon, attack!" Seavig yelled.

He led his men as he grabbed onto the thick ropes and slid his way down to the ground, right before their own ship toppled in the mud. He drew his sword and charged across the muddy ground, his men joining him.

The Pandesians met them in the middle in a great clash of weaponry. Seavig raised his sword high and threw himself into the group of Pandesians, slashing two men at a time, not even slowing to raise his shield. He wheeled around and smashed one with the hilt of his sword in the nose, stabbed another, spun and elbowed a third, and kicked a fourth. He fought like a man possessed, cutting his way through the ranks of the Pandesian soldiers.

Yet still, he and his men were surrounded. Thousands of Pandesian soldiers collected themselves and they were quickly outmanned ten to one in a hand-to-hand battle. He knew they would not last long. They would die here, after all, ironically on foot in a muddy seabed.

There arose a sudden shout and Seavig looked around, confused, wondering where it came from. Then he saw it, high up in the bell towers, in the re-emerging buildings of Ur. There, he was shocked to see, were groups of warriors, men of Ur who had ridden out the flood, had taken refuge in the high ground. Seavig had not noticed them before, but as the city's water drained lower and lower, he watched as dozens of these men clambered down the buildings, down to the muddy ground of the city of Ur. They let out a great battle cry as they charged across the dry harbor to attack the Pandesians.

The Pandesians turned, caught off guard, and that gave Seavig the precious momentum he needed. He and his men attacked, while the surviving warriors of Ur attacked the Pandesians from the other side. The Pandesians did not know which way to fight first, and soon, sandwiched between them, they fell by the dozens.

Seavig fought and fought until his shoulders grew tired, never relenting until he had no one left to fight.

Finally he stopped and looked around, breathing hard, amazed at the silence. He watched as his men embraced the men of Ur, as he heard shouts of victory rise to the sky, and he realized something, with a gush of relief.

The battle was over.

Ur, once again, was free.

CHAPTER TWENTY NINE

Kyra raced through the skies, gripping Theon's scales, a bird's-eye view of the desert beneath her as they dove down, her stomach plummeting, to the other side of the Devil's Gulch. Gripping the Staff of Truth, Kyra dove down past the steep cliffs, the ocean waves crashing on the other side, and she was no longer overwhelmed by sadness. Her sadness had been replaced by a new emotion: vengeance. Cold, steely vengeance.

It was time to defeat Pandesia once and for all, to set wrongs right in Escalon. Too long had her people been oppressed; for too long had they not stood up to this nation, not risked their lives to make their land free. Finally, the day had come, the day her ancestors had dreamt about, had prophesied for a thousand years. As she flew, leading her people, she felt as if she were making history.

Kyra heard the distant shouts and looked down to see her father's army below, hundreds of men charging down the other side of the Gulch, all following her as she led the way. She looked up and saw the thousands of Pandesians up ahead, spread out in the wasteland south of the Gulch, all assembling in columns and clearly preparing for a counter-attack. They stretched to the horizon, covering her land, all the way to the Bridge of Sorrows, an entire nation bent on destroying and retaking Escalon.

Kyra dove lower, gripping Theon around his neck with one hand and the staff with the other, and she could feel the rage pulsing through him, too.

"This is our time, Theon," she whispered, feeling at one with her dragon. "This is the day we were both born for."

He roared in response and flew faster, needing no urging. He dove lower, opened his jaws, and as the first legion of soldiers entered their sights, he roared a column of fire.

A huge wave of fire rolled down, spreading out below, Kyra able to feel the heat even from here. The Pandesian soldiers looked up in terror, as if watching a nightmare descend from the skies. They turned to flee—but it was too late. They were all stuck in the fishbowl below, hundreds of thousands of their fellow soldiers blocking their escape.

Theon's flames engulfed them, and a chorus of shrieks arose as a great fire roared through the crowd. It wiped out hundreds of men at a time, stumbling, collapsing to their knees, turning to ash. Kyra felt a deep satisfaction with each death.

"LOWER!" she urged.

They flew even lower, until they were but feet from the flames, Kyra seeing all the detail up close. She wanted to get closer and closer to the fire, to feel its heat, to feel firsthand the vengeance she was giving her father. She came so close that the heat hurt her face, and yet still she would not pull up. Hardly ten feet above their heads, she watched as men, on fire, were shrieking, collapsing, some trying to hurl spears up at the dragon, but being killed before they could even let go.

Horns sounded, and Kyra looked out and saw, in the distance, columns of soldiers rallying, preparing to make a stand against her. Horns sounded again and again as thousands of men on horses, on elephants, in chariots, on foot, charged to meet her and Theon.

Kyra lowered her head, welcoming the challenge.

"FASTER, THEON!"

They flew so fast she could hardly breathe, closing in on the bulk of the army, and as they did, the soldiers below, prepared, hurled spears, fired arrows, sent up an army of weaponry into the skies, all intent on killing her and Theon.

Kyra did not flinch. Instead, she raised the Staff of Truth and, as she felt it vibrating in her hand, slashed it downwards.

A column of black light descended, and as it went, it knocked the spears and arrows out of the skies.

A creaking noise cut through the air and Kyra looked down to see several catapults being rolled forward. Ropes were cut, and a moment later, boulders were soaring through the air, right for her. Just one of these boulders, she knew, could fell Theon.

Kyra held out the staff before her, and she felt an intense power as light shot down from it. The light hit the rocks mid-air and smashed them to pieces, raining down chunks of rock on all the soldiers, and knocking them unconscious by the dozens.

Kyra heard a rallying cry behind her, and she glanced back to see Anvin leading the men, hunting down the Pandesians that fled in every direction. She soared with pride as she watched the men on horseback raise swords and shields, and fell rows of Pandesian soldiers—those foolish enough to turn around and make a stand. Anvin and the others fought like men possessed, all clearly on a mission to avenge her father. They threw themselves fearlessly into the enemy and hacked them down, carving out a path right down the middle of the Pandesian forces.

Their efforts distracted the Pandesians and helped Kyra stay on track as she dove again and again, criss-crossing, sending columns of flame down across the army. All the while, though, she was hunting single-mindedly for one man.

Ra.

Kyra scoured the ranks as she flew, desperate to find his golden chariot. She had a debt to settle. Her father's blood demanded it.

Kyra flew farther and farther south, taking out legions of soldiers as Theon breathed fire. She was determined to clear a path all the way to the Bridge of Sorrows, to the very end of the land of Escalon, and to kill every last one. When she was done, she would circle back and kill whoever remained. She would attack as long as she needed to until her land was finally free again.

Kyra cut a wide swath through the army, the flames rippling down, shouts filling the air, knowing she had to reach the Bridge of Sorrows before Ra could escape. She could not leave him alive to regroup, to fight another day. If he crossed that bridge, he could rally millions more soldiers from greater Pandesia, and Escalon could be invaded once again, an endless flood invading her homeland forever. She would have to, she realized, take out the Bridge of Sorrows altogether. There was no other way. She could not leave her homeland open to be invaded once again.

Kyra flew and flew, Theos burning fire all the while, the flames roaring below, sending up clouds of smoke, until finally her heart beat faster as she spotted it in the distance: the Bridge of Sorrows. There it sat, shining in the sun, an ancient and iconic piece of architecture, crowned by the Southern Gate, built by her ancestors, rising hundreds of feet above the ocean, spanning the two continents, connecting Escalon to the mainland of Pandesia. Kyra could even see beyond it, all the way to the black Fields of Ore gleaming on the opposite side, the northernmost tip of the massive landmass of the Pandesian Empire, stretching beyond it to the end of the world.

Kyra was confused as she saw tens of thousands of Pandesian soldiers gathering before the gate. It was as if they did not want to cross—but rather to make a stand. As if they were waiting for something. And then, her heart pounded as she saw the man she had been looking for. There stood Ra, alone on the bridge, awaiting her.

Only his sorcerer, Magon, stood beside him, while assembled before him, on the mainland, were Pandesia's elite legions.

"DOWN, THEON!"

As Kyra neared, she felt sure she was flying into a trap. Yet she would not back down for anything. On the contrary: she was determined to dismount, and to face Ra on foot, and to kill him by hand.

As she neared, close enough to see their faces, Magon raised his dark scarlet staff toward the sky. A moment later, Kyra felt a burning in her palm, and she looked down and was dismayed to watch the Staff of Truth losing its glow. Magon was somehow neutralizing its power.

At the same moment, Theon's flames suddenly stopped, as if slamming into an invisible wall in the air, before the bridge. She saw Magon raising his arms, eyes closed, and realized he was casting some sort of spell to take away both of their powers. As if he were summoning something.

And then it came: a roar. Not just a roar, but the loudest sound she had ever heard, rumbling through the skies, piercing her ears. Kyra looked up, and saw the most frightening thing she had ever seen. Four creatures, resembling dragons but ten times the size, flew toward her. Their scales were black, their eyes, as large as she, black, too, with glowing yellow slits. Their bodies were lumpy, misshapen, and long yellow talons hung down from their feet. They came from the four corners of the sky, all converging for her. They were creatures summoned from hell.

Kyra was proud that Theon did not shrink in fear; even without his flames, he was enraged, and lunged forward to meet them in battle. These creatures, though, were too fast; barely had she spotted them when they were already upon her, reaching out with their talons for her, converging all at once.

Kyra swung the Staff of Truth—yet this time, stripped of its power, it did no good. Within moments the creatures were all on Theon, tearing at him in four directions. Kyra struggled to hold on as his body rocked wildly, Theon fighting viciously. As small as he was, he refused to go down without a fight. He snapped at their throats, slashed at their eyes. But their scales were like armor, and he hardly made a scratch.

One of them clamped down on Theon's tail and jerked his head, and as he did, Theon was thrown through the skies. Kyra felt her stomach dropping, her world spinning out of control as Theon plummeted head over heels through the air. Kyra held on as long as she could, knowing she needed to be close to the ground before she fell.

Finally, she fell, shrieking as she descended through the air, praying she was not so high that the fall would kill her.

She hit the ground with a thud, realizing, luckily, that she had been only twenty feet above when she lost her grip. She landed on the bridge, feeling a cracking in her ribs, and she lay there, winded. A moment later Theon crashed, smashing into the ground on the far side of the bridge, desperately wounded, trying to flap his wings but unable.

The four creatures peered down and began to dive for him, to finish him off.

At the same time Kyra heard a dark chanting, and she forced herself to lift her head, and looked out to see Magon standing on the far side of the bridge, raising both arms, emitting an awful noise. As he did, Kyra sensed motion behind him, and her heart stopped to see the Fields of Ore were changing. The blackened fields were bubbling, rising up, as if the stones themselves were coming alive. She watched in horror as a sea of blackened monsters suddenly emerged from the rock, standing tall. They marched across the Fields of Ore, heading for the Bridge of Sorrows, preparing to enter Escalon. The sorcerer was raising an army of the dead.

Kyra slowly rose to her feet, her entire body aching, forcing herself up, using the Staff of Truth to prop her. She stood there and faced off against Ra, against his sorcerer, while their army of the dead approached.

Ra stepped forward and smiled.

"Finally," he said to her, "our time has come."

CHAPTER THIRTY

Lorna watched with admiration and concern as Merk boarded the Pandesian ship and attacked its men. She watched with pride as he moved their cannon before they fired, saving Seavig, giving them the chance they needed to finish securing the chain, to close off the harbor. It was heroic and selfless, and Lorna had not realized that Merk had it in him. He had made amends, in that moment, for past wrongs, for a life poorly led. She felt true love for him.

She had wanted to join him, to be by his side, yet she could not, still busy as she was in keeping her palms to the sky, in creating the mist to obscure the Pandesian fleet. It was Merk's fight, and he was on his own. It was his struggle for redemption.

She watched as, finally, in that last moment, he had found it. Lorna looked away as Merk was killed, encircled and stabbed by the Pandesians. She had felt it herself, in every ounce of her body, like a knife entering her own gut.

She cried out in despair.

Finished with her mist, Lorna saw that Seavig, safely in the harbor, no longer needed her. She was finally free to turn to Merk. She steered her ship for the Pandesian ship where she knew Merk lay dead. She sailed through an ocean full of Pandesian ships, many on fire all around her, others covered in mist, and others still splintering, falling apart as they sailed into the spiked chains. A sickening cracking noise filled the air, along with the screams of thousands of dying men. It was a night of hell for the Pandesians, and a night of epic victory for Escalon.

Yet still a few ships remained, including this one on which Merk lay dead. As her boat touched its hull, Lorna ran forward, leapt into the air, and used her powers to lift herself, to bridge the ten-foot gap easily. She landed like a cat on the Pandesian ship, to the amazed stares of all the soldiers.

Lorna strutted slowly, proudly, down the center of the deck, unafraid as soldiers turned toward her and stared, unsure whether to welcome or kill her. There she was, a woman alone walking down their ship, unafraid, looking like an apparition. The soldiers stared at each other, clearly baffled, unsure what to make of her.

Finally one of them raised his sword high and charged her.

Lorna merely flicked her palm and summoned her power, and his sword stopped in mid-air. She waved her wrist, and the soldier and sword went flying sideways through the air, overboard, splashing into the waters below.

The soldiers all now charged her. They drew swords, wielded maces, came at her with everything they had. The result was the same for them all: their blows were stopped by the invisible shield she spun around herself. Flicking her wrist, she sent men flying up into the air and over the sides of the ship, into the sea.

As she walked, calm, unfazed, she created a path of destruction. Soon the ship was emptied of Pandesians, all floating in the waters below, being eaten by sharks.

Lorna looked out to the horizon and saw the remainder of the Pandesian fleet in the ocean, hundreds of ships still anchored there, able to stop themselves before reaching the spiked chains. She reached back with her palms, threw them forward, and huge, white balls of light flew through the air like boulders. They lit up the night as they flew far out to sea, finally landing in the waters with a great crash.

Enormous waves arose and lifted the remaining Pandesian ships, sending them surging toward the harbor, toward Seavig's spiked chains. Whatever ships had survived were soon destroyed.

Lorna breathed easy for the first time. The sea was finally free of Pandesian ships.

Lorna hurried to the bow, finally reaching Merk, kneeling by his side. There he lay, prone, eyes open wide to the sky. Frozen.

Dead.

Blood leaked from the wound in his stomach, and her heart broke at the sight of him. This scarred man, who had managed to redeem himself, to become a fine man in the final moments of his life, now lay there, dead before his time. It was as if his true personality had always been waiting for its chance to emerge.

"Merk," she said softly, crying.

Lorna placed one hand on his stomach, and the other over his eyes, closing them. She felt a tremendous heat burning in her palms, and as she closed her eyes, she could feel his spirit leaving him, hovering, overlooking them both.

"Stay here with me," she said to his spirit. "Let us start a new life together. I am ready now. And I am not ready to lose you."

Lorna closed her eyes and began to feel Merk's energy coursing through her with fervor. She could feel Merk's soul struggling, debating if he wanted to stay. He was a tired soul, one who had lived a life of anguish, and his spirit hovered in the balance. It was a decision only he could make.

She watched his eyes flutter, hoping they would open. She had no idea if they would.

CHAPTER THIRTY ONE

Alec sprinted across the peninsula of Ur, the Unfinished Sword urging him on, showing him which way to go. He knew he was running headlong into danger, and he did not care. He felt his destiny before him, the destiny of Escalon hanging in the balance, and today was the day, he knew, that would define his life.

Seeing Dierdre back there, together with his best friend, Marco, had done something to him. In some ways, it had made him lose his will to live. Though he barely knew her, he had loved Dierdre more than he could say, more than he had ever loved anyone, more than he had even realized until now. He had loved Marco as a friend, too. Seeing the two of them together, seeing how much they loved each other, was like a double knife in his heart. He had thought all this time that when he returned to her, she would be awaiting him. No matter what happened to him, it was all going to be worth it as long as he was reunited with her again.

But seeing that she no longer loved him, it robbed him of his will to live.

Alec sprinted across the barren, windswept peninsula, running for the mountain of rubble in the distance that was once the Tower of Ur. He looked out and saw Alva in the distance, holding out his staff, creating a fissure in the earth in which hundreds of vicious trolls fell. Yet he also saw dozens more trolls breaking through, charging the rubble—and atop it, he saw a lone figure, a man he immediately recognized as Kolva, fighting them all off heroically. The Unfinished Sword hummed in his hand, and Alec knew immediately that that was where he was needed.

Kolva stood atop the rubble, swinging his staff, knocking out trolls two, three, four at a time, while Leo snarled viciously at his feet, and Andor trampled trolls behind him, all of them tearing apart trolls on all sides. Alec could not understand what he was doing there. It was as if he were guarding the pile of rubble. Was this where Alec was meant to go?

Despite his confusion, Alec let the sword lead him; it practically pulled him and he ran by and in a blur he saw the chaos all around him, saw thousands of trolls pouring in every second. He saw Alva's arms shaking as he held his staff, barely able to hold his fissure any longer. He saw trees dropped, bridges erected, the fissure overrun by more and more trolls. Soon, he could tell, Alva and Kolva, the last thing keeping the trolls at bay, would be overrun for good.

Alec ran for the rubble, so close now—when suddenly he felt a yank, and felt a surge of pain as his arm was clawed. He cried out and spun to find a grotesque troll bearing down on him. Without thinking, Alec spun and slashed the troll across the chest, letting the sword lead him, then drove it into his heart, killing him. The sword cut through him as if he weren't even there.

Another troll lunged for Alec from the other direction, and he ducked, letting it fly over him, then slashed its back, killing it.

Alec ran, breathing hard, stumbling over the mounds of rubble, dodging trolls, until finally he was at Kolva's side. He fought back to back with him, each slashing back trolls, Alec with his sword, Kolva with his staff.

Kolva glanced down at the weapon in Alec's hand. His eyes widened with reverence.

"The sword," he gasped.

Alec looked back, wondering.

"You know where it belongs?" Alec asked.

"The secret chamber," Kolva replied. "Deep beneath the earth. Kyle awaits you below. You must go now. Hurry!"

As Kolva uttered the words, Alec immediately knew them to be true, and his mission snapped into focus. He looked down at the pile of rubble beneath his feet, and he saw the opening not far away, leading down into the earth. It was the final resting place of the Sword. And the only way, he realized, to save Escalon.

Alec prepared to go, but Kolva reached out and placed a firm hand on his shoulder. He gave him a somber look.

"The chamber," he said, "when you restore the sword, it will swallow it whole. And *you* with it. Whatever's left of this tower will be no more. There will be no return."

Alec stood there, pondering Kyle's words. The ultimate sacrifice, he realized, was not only returning the sword, but sacrificing himself. A quest awaited him, and it was a quest for martyrs. One for the man who was willing to end his life for the sake of Escalon.

As Alec felt the sword hum in his hand, he knew what he had to do.

"Then time is short," he replied.

With those words, Alec ran and leapt through the hole.

His stomach dropped as he plummeted into a world of blackness. He landed hard, stumbled, found his feet, and immediately set off at a run in the darkness, his way lit only by a distant torch. He followed a maze of corridors, allowing the sword to lead him, until finally he reached the end, an open, glowing door before him.

And before it, a single figure.

Kyle.

Kyle turned and looked at him, awe in his face.

"The ancient chamber," Kyle breathed.

Alec felt the sword burning, red-hot, in his palms, and he knew.

"This is my mission now," Alec said. "You have done your job well. Surface. And serve Escalon as best you can."

Kyle stared back, concern and admiration in his face. He stepped forward and they clasped arms solemnly.

"Escalon shall always remember you," Kyle said.

And with that, he turned and hurried back through the corridors, leaving Alec utterly alone.

Alec knew he was meant to be here, and knew he was meant to be alone. His breathing shallow, he stepped into the chamber, knowing this would be the last room he ever stepped in.

The chamber was bright, aglow with torches, and as he entered, the sword was positively vibrating in his hand. This place, the absolute silence, the stillness in the air, felt sacrosanct. He stepped in deeper and looked around. In the center was a round, granite altar. And in its very center was a slit, a scabbard embedded in the stone. It was the same size and shape of the sword. He knew at once that that was where the sword was meant to live. Forever. It would finish the sword. And it would finish Escalon.

Alec stepped forward, his heart pounding, knowing these were his final moments alive. He felt a great sense of tragedy, of sadness—yet also of purpose, of honor. Hearing the shouts above, he knew it was time. Time to end this war. To restore the Flames. To send the trolls back to Marda. Forever.

Alec stepped close and uttered his final words.

"Dierdre," he said. "I love you."

Alec raised the sword high with both hands and plunged it down into the slit in the earth.

The sword turn red-hot, aglow, and Alec stepped away, its power too intense. Flames shot up from the rock, there came the sound of stone scraping stone, and suddenly, the entire world began to quake.

Rubble began collapsing all around him. And his final thought, as his world turned black, as massive boulders collapsed atop him, was: *Escalon, I have served you.*

CHAPTER THIRTY TWO

Alva stood before the fissure, holding his staff before him, and he could feel his power waning. His arms shook from the hours of effort, and yet still the trolls came, thousands and thousands more, a never-ending river of monsters. Alva knew time was of the essence, now more than ever, and yet, his powers had reached their end. He could not hold them back much longer. The fate of Escalon no longer rested on him, but now, on the Unfinished Sword. If Kyle and Kolva and Alec could restore it in time, then they'd have a chance. If not, all was lost.

Alva struggled with all he had, and yet despite all his efforts, he could no longer hold up his arms. They lowered by themselves, his staff dimming, and as they dropped, he watched with horror as the fissure began to seal again.

There came a great roar as thousands of trolls, invigorated, jumped over the closing fissure, charging right for him. At the same time, the trolls overwhelmed Kyle and Kolva on the rubble of the tower, swarming them from all sides. Their battle, he knew, was lost.

There came yet another shout, and Alva spun and was horrified to see Vesuvius himself appear, surprising him, charging him from behind as he led thousands more trolls. Vesuvius had clearly circled around and waited for the perfect moment to attack. In that moment, Alva knew his life, after centuries on this planet, was over. He could no longer withstand an attack by an entire nation of trolls on his own.

Alva wielded his staff as the first wave of trolls came, stepping forward and slashing. With a great cracking noise he knocked a dozen of them back in a single blow. He spun and swung again, and felled more.

Yet still they came, thousands upon thousands, snarling, eyes red, filled with bloodlust. Even Kyle and Kolva could not hold them back anymore—they deflected deadly blows with their staffs, but then they stumbled and fell, overwhelmed. At the same time, Vesuvius broke through the ranks, rushing forward and setting his sights on Alva. Alva watched as Vesuvius raised his immense halberd high and lowered it for his head.

Alva raised his staff, turned it sideways, and blocked it—yet as he did, he heard the sickening noise of his staff cracking in two. Alva stared at the broken shards in disbelief. That which could not be broken had been broken. That could only mean one thing: the heart and soul of Escalon was broken, too. There was no hope left for any of them.

Vesuvius grinned and raised his halberd again, and this time, Alva knew the next blow would kill him.

Alva did not try to resist. He had lived long enough to meet his fate calmly when it came for him. He stood there proudly, greeting the end of his life not with fear, but with resolve. If that was what the universe wanted of him, then so be it.

As Vesuvius stepped forward, suddenly, Alva stumbled, as the earth quaked beneath him. The quaking grew more intense, and Vesuvius and the trolls stumbled along with him. It was a tremendous earthquake, gaining in strength, feeling as if the entire core of the earth were being shook.

Alva fell to the ground, the thousands of trolls with him, wondering what was happening as he tried to regain his equilibrium. And then, suddenly, he realized. The Unfinished Sword. It had been returned to its home. Kyle, Kolva, and Alec had succeeded.

The earth shook and shook, as if all of Escalon were being reborn, and suddenly, there followed a great hissing noise. Alva looked to the north and already on the horizon he could see the glow, growing brighter by the second.

The Flames were being restored.

Alva heard a rumbling, and he looked over and watched the rubble of the tower collapsing upon itself. All that remained of the tower was sinking into the earth. Kyle and Kolva leapt out of the way just in time, before being sucked down with it.

They rushed to his side, as Alva regained his feet and began to feel his own energy return. The three of them raised their staffs, and as one, they all faced off with Vesuvius.

Vesuvius stumbled to his feet and stared back, wide-eyed. For the first time, Alva saw real fear on his face. Clearly, he had not expected this. In the distance, the air was filled with the shrieks of his troll nation, millions of them, being burned alive as they migrated south and were trapped in the new Wall of Flames. Behind them came the cries of millions more trolls, now trapped behind the Flames, trapped in Marda forever, their dreams of invading Escalon crushed for good.

Vesuvius clearly realized in that moment that he was trapped here now, on this side of the Flames, cut off from his nation, his army. That all his hopes and dreams were crushed. That all that remained of his troll army were these few thousands, trapped here inside of Escalon. All demoralized, all knowing they had lost, that they could never return to Marda.

Alva reached out his arms, and as he did, his staff rose in the air and came back together, the two parts mending perfectly as he regained his strength. He, too, felt reborn. Beside him, Kolva and Kyle raised their staffs, and the three of them, with a new energy, faced off with Vesuvius.

Vesuvius raised his halberd, uncertain for the first time. He stared back at them all in shock as the three of them charged. Alva swung first, knocking the halberd from his hands, while Kolva swung his staff and cracked him in the chest. Kyle stepped up and kicked him, knocking him down.

As he lay there, defenseless, Magon stepped forward out of the mist, and rose his palm towards Alva.

Alva nodded to Kyle and Kolva and they turned and ran off into the crowd, pursuing the other trolls as they tried to escape back to the Flames.

Magon stepped forward, and raised his palm, scowling, as if to kill Alva.

But Alva, feeling more powerful than ever, merely stepped forward, took Magon's hand in his, made a fist and crushed it. Magon shrieked, yet it did little good. Alva kicked him, sending him flying back thirty feet, into the closing fissure, with an awful shriek from hell. Dead.

Alva alone stepped forward and faced Vesuvius. This was his battle to fight. His and his alone.

*

Vesuvius felt a wave of panic for the first time in his life. As he watched the Flames restored, he knew it was over. Everything he had fought for, had lived for, had fallen apart. The Flames, inexplicably, had somehow risen again. This, he had never foreseen. And now, this was a battle he could not win.

Seeing Alva bearing down on him, Vesuvius scrambled to his hands and knees, turned, and for the first time in his life, he fled.

Alva pursued him. As Vesuvius ran, he watched Kyle and Kolva charge into the trolls and swing ferociously, driving what remained of his nation all back, north, for the Flames. His trolls, demoralized, fled, trying foolishly to return to Marda. They all shrieked and fell as Kyle and Kolva caught up with them, felling them one at a time.

Vesuvius ran, too, senselessly back toward Marda, knowing there was no way out yet needing to see it for himself, to see the Flames up close. He burst through a patch of woods, Alva on his heels, and finally he stopped in shock as the great Flames roared before him, glowing, sparking. He could feel their heat on his face even from here.

He stood there staring, aghast. It was true. The Flames had risen once again. His nation was cut off from Escalon, this time, he sensed, for good.

Vesuvius watched as Kyle and Kolva swung their staffs ferociously, smashing trolls on every side, killing them dozens at a time as they sent them into the Flames. No one could stand up to their power, and his trolls were too terrified to do anything but attempt to run back home.

A few trolls finally stopped at the Flames, turned around, and put up a fight. But it was half-hearted. Kyle and Kolva fought like men possessed, destroying what remained of his nation in a dizzying whirl of prowess. He watched them knock out twenty trolls before even one could raise a halberd.

Vesuvius finally stopped himself. He turned, his back to the Flames, cornered in, and faced Alva.

Alva approached calmly, staff before him, as if cornering a wounded deer. Vesuvius stood there, and he felt ready. He was ready to make amends for his lifetime of crimes, for all the raping and pillaging and murder, for all the pain and agony he had inflicted on others. He knew this day would come. He had just not expected it so soon.

Vesuvius felt a deep regret and shame. He had failed all of Marda, as had his forefathers before him. The trolls would never have Escalon. They would always be contained in Marda.

Yet Vesuvius had one last flash of anger, of defiance. If he was going to die, it would be on *his* terms. He wouldn't let Alva have the satisfaction.

As Alva approached, Vesuvius, with one final battle cry, turned and threw himself into the Wall of Flames. He shrieked as he felt himself burning, being consumed alive. He felt demons descending, taking his soul, preparing to drag it into the darkest depths of hell and tear it to bits.

His agony, he knew, had just begun.

CHAPTER THIRTY THREE

Kavos led his men up the icy cliffs of Kos, all of them clinging to the side of the mountain with their ice picks, barely managing to hang in the face of howling winds. Kavos, swaying after a particularly strong gust, glanced over to see Bramthos beside him, and hundreds of his men below, all climbing as fast as they could to beat out the Pandesian army.

The air was filled with the chorus of ice chipping, with the sound of arrowheads and spearheads chipping the ice wall, rising even above the wind, cast by the Pandesians. Kavos looked down and was relieved to see they were out of range of now. The Pandesian army, unable to climb like they could, were powerless at the bottom, only able to fire arrows that fell short or were diverted in the wind. After all, these mountains were for the men of Kos, and the men of Kos were not faint of heart.

Kavos craned his neck and looked back to the horizon and saw the ground filled with men, tens of thousands of them, the entire northern legion of the Pandesian army. Though he had but several hundred men at his disposal, he was unafraid. This, after all, was his terrain. He remembered what his father had once told him: *Terrain, not manpower, won wars.*

If Duncan could manage to kill the entire southern legion of the Pandesian army in the Gulch, and if Seavig could manage to destroy the Pandesian fleet in Ur, then the final battle against the Pandesians would be waged here, Kavos knew, in these icy mountains of Kos. If he and his men could win this battle, then they would rid the land of the last of the Pandesians, and Escalon would be free once again. It was a dream he harbored with all his heart— and he was determined to make it happen.

Kavos knew what was at stake, and he did not hesitate as he climbed higher and higher, despite his shaking arms, his numb hands, scaling his way up the cliffs like a goat. His muscles burned, tore at him from every side; he could no longer feel his nose, his cheeks, yet still, he did not stop climbing. He would rest when he was dead.

Finally, he reached a broad plateau of ice jutting out from the cliff, the halfway point to his home high above. He collapsed for a moment, lying on it gratefully, arms shaking, as all the others caught up with him. They all lay there, catching their breath, relieved to be alive in the howling wind.

Kavos finally gained his feet, nodded to his men, and they raised long, curved horns from their waists, leaned back, and blew.

It was the sound he remembered, the special horns reserved for the warriors of Kos, horns which only fellow men of Kos would understand. The sound echoed over the very cliffs, reaching every contour.

As they sounded them, there came a great rumbling high above. It was the rest of his warriors, he knew, the ones he had left behind to guard his homeland, to act as reserves when the time came. Kavos looked up and as he knew he would, saw hundreds of his men, dressed in battle furs, grabbing their ropes and quickly rappelling down the face of the icy cliffs. They moved like lightning, all heeding his call. They wielded the long, sharp instruments of his people, special weapons forged for centuries by the men of Kos. They resembled pikes, twenty feet long, with long, shiny silver handles and pronged, steel-reinforced tips. They were built to withstand the cold, and to puncture the one thing they had in abundance: ice.

Within moments, they landed beside him, hundreds of men, joining his men on the broad plateau, tripling the size of his force. His men embraced.

Kavos felt all eyes on him. He walked to the edge, joined by Bramthos, and looked down the cliffs. He watched the tens of thousands of Pandesians below pathetically try to climb the cliff. Most slid back two feet for every foot they gained. Yet still, they were foolish enough to come.

"Man the shelf!" Kavos commanded, shouting over the wind.

His men spread out and ran to the edge of the plateau, each grabbing a pike. Kavos grabbed one, too, admiring the weight of the long silver staff. All the others carried the long, heavy instruments in groups of two, but Kavos needed only himself.

Its weight was tremendous, but Kavos finally managed to hoist it to the edge of the cliff. He stood there, face against the howling wind, and he looked left and right to check his men's positions. He looked up at the massive icicles overhead, hundreds of them, some of them fifty feet long and just as thick. All of them pointing straight down, an overhang over the cliff, like weapons of death. These icicles of death were the crop of Kos.

Kavos looked back down at the Pandesians below, still climbing, oblivious to what was about to come. The time had come to let the terrain do the fighting for him. All his life he had prepared for a day like this.

"NOW!" he cried.

With a shout his men rushed forth with their pikes, Kavos leading the way, Bramthos beside him, and they stabbed the great icicles clinging to the side of the cliff. Kavos stabbed again and again, until the pronged tip began to puncture the thick slabs of ice. Soon, a sharp cracking noise began to spread.

All around them icicles began to separate and fall. There came a whooshing noise, and Kavos felt a great wind rush past.

Kavos looked down and watched as the stalactites fell on the first wave of Pandesian soldiers. Even above the howling of the wind, shrieks began to fill the air. Hundreds of them, halfway up the cliffs, cried out and fell as they were pierced by the ice. Hundreds more, gathered below, were crushed by falling ice and bodies.

Again and again the icicles fell, landing far below with explosions that shook the world, even up here. An avalanche formed as immense ice boulders broke off the mountain and began to roll into the army. Thousands more fled, but not in time, crushed by the mountain of ice and snow.

The Pandesians, panicked, sounded horns and retreated from the mountain face, clearly stunned by the loss of so many men so quickly.

Kavos would not give them time.

"The ice shelf!" Kavos yelled. "Now!"

His men ran all the way to the very edge of the icy plateau they were standing on and, following Kavos's lead, each man grabbed a rope. They then raised their pikes high and smashed them down on the very shelf they had been standing on.

All at once, the shelf gave way, the massive plateau separating from the mountainside. It fell not straight down, but leaned over sideways, a huge slab of ice, falling far out from the mountain face, like a pancake, coming right down for the Pandesian forces.

Kavos felt the weight of it disappear from beneath him, and with suddenly nothing left to stand on, he held on tight to the rope, as did his men around him. Dangling in mid-air, he looked and watched the entire shelf land on thousands more soldiers, crushing them with a great cloud of ice and snow. There followed an awful rumbling as an enormous cloud of ice spread like a wave, engulfing the rest of the Pandesian army. They tried to run, but could not outrun it. As Kavos watched, thousands more men were crushed.

The Pandesian army was now entirely in panic and disarray. Kavos would not give them time to reassemble.

"MEN!" cried Kavos. "WE FIGHT!"

There came a great cheer as his men joined him in rappelling down the mountain. They slid down to the ground in no time, ran across the ice, and made right for the scattered Pandesian forces.

Kavos hurled a javelin, sending it skidding along the ice, and it took out three soldiers, puncturing their legs, before it even slowed.

All around him his men hurled spears, taking out dozens of soldiers. They soon closed the gap on the fleeing soldiers, and as they did Kavos drew his sword and threw himself into the enemy, as did the men around him.

They hit the Pandesians like a tidal wave, his several hundred men attacking an army in shock, an army still reeling from the avalanche. Some Pandesians tried to put up a fight, but they slipped on the snow and ice, not used to the terrain as the men of Kos were. They could barely raise a sword against the men of Kos, who hacked down man after man after man as they tore through the remaining forces like a whirlwind.

In but moments, thousands of Pandesians were felled—and the ones who were not, turned and fled.

"Catapults!" Kavos commanded.

His men sounded their horns, this time in a series of short blasts, and they were answered by horns high atop the cliffs. Barely had the answer come when the sky was suddenly filled with the sound of whistling. Kavos did not need to look up to know what it was, but he craned his neck anyway to watch: his other men, high above, as commanded, were unleashing the catapults of ice.

Before them huge boulders of ice fell from the sky like hail, each the size of ten men. Explosions followed, the first with enough power to make the earth quake and send Kavos stumbling off his feet.

Within moments, what remained of the Pandesian army was decimated.

Finally, the catapults stopped, and Kavos cried: "CHARGE!"

Kavos led his men on a charge through the remnants of the army, killing any dazed soldiers they found left.

Before long Kavos reached the Pandesian commander personally, one of the last men alive. The coward turned and ran, and Kavos hurled a sword at his back.

It impaled him, and he fell face first and went skidding across the ice.

Dead.

Kavos's men let out a great cheer. It was a cheer of victory. A cheer of vengeance. The northern army had been routed.

Escalon was free again.

CHAPTER THIRTY FOUR

Kyra stood alone on the vast Bridge of Sorrows, facing off against Ra in the battle that she knew would determine her fate. She stood there, wielding the Staff of Truth, determined to avenge her father. Ra stood across from her, equally determined as he raised his huge golden sword high. Kyra sensed that the outcome of this fight would determine not only her own fate, but the fate of Escalon as well. This, she sensed, was the final battle of the entire war, the battle her father never had a chance to complete.

Behind Ra, countless thousands of black monsters were rising from the soil, crossing the Fields of Ore, his sorcerer summoning them from the depths of hell. Above her the four immense dragon-like creatures pierced the air with their shrieks, diving down for Theon. Kyra saw her dragon lying there on the ground, and she wished more than ever she could come to his aid. But he would have to be on his own. She had her own battle to wage.

Behind her the mainland was filled with the sound of shouts, of men dying, as Anvin led what remained of Duncan's army, attacking the Pandesian forces despite their overwhelming number, immersing themselves in the greatest war of Escalon's history. All of them had put their lives on the line, and all of their lives hung in the balance. Kyra felt an extra sense of urgency to reunite with them and help them finish the battle.

Kyra wanted to be everywhere at once. She wanted to be fighting with her father's men, and she wanted to be defending Theon—yet she knew that they each had a role to play, and her role was here, on the bridge, facing off against Ra, his sorcerer, and the legions of monsters behind them. Her role was to defend the Bridge of Sorrows, the entry to Escalon, for once and for all. She felt the staff throbbing in her hand, and she knew the time had come.

Kyra stood there, prepared for Ra to step forward and fight.

Yet to her surprise, he merely grinned wide and stepped aside.

As he did there arose a horrific moaning noise, and Kyra looked out to see the thousands of black creatures leaving the Fields of Ore, entering the bridge, charging her. Ra clearly wanted them to do the fighting for him.

Kyra was amazed at Ra's cowardice as she watched the beasts run past him, right for her. His sorcerer grinned, too, each smug in their evil, each watching, waiting for these demons to do their dirty work for them. She braced herself, ready for the challenge. This was, after all, a war of good versus evil, of humanity against demons, of freedom versus tyranny. This battle was just the final manifestation of what had always lurked beneath the surface.

Kyra thought of her dead father, his noble face in death burned in her mind. She could not give up, not now, no matter how badly the odds were stacked against her. Even if the staff failed her, even if her powers failed her, she would not give up. She was, after all, a warrior in her own right, and she had her own two hands to fight with. That was all she'd ever wanted in life.

Kyra charged, not waiting for her foes to reach her. She raised the Staff of Truth and swung wildly, marking the first impact of the battle as she smashed the first black creature that came her way. It was an awful thing, twice her size, made of a black sticky substance, like clay, dripping, with small red eyes and rows of sharp, yellow teeth. It was a creature that never should have existed.

As Kyra slashed it across the midsection, her staff became lost in a glob of black tar, sending it exploding all around her. Another creature lunged and grabbed her arm, while another grabbed for her other arm. Kyra did not hesitate—she spun, raised the staff, and cracked one across its chest, then jabbed the other between the eyes, exploding both all over the bridge.

Kyra leapt into the crowd, swinging her staff like a warrior possessed. She spun and swung, ducking, rising, lowering her staff and bringing it up. She slashed and fought like lightning as she passed through the crowd, lost in a blur as these creatures clawed at her and exploded all around her. Kyra let all her instincts, all her training, take over her as she let the staff guide her. She barely had a sense of what she was doing as she surrendered to the control of the universe, as she truly let go and allowed herself to get lost in the whirlwind of battle.

Kyra felled one creature after the next, their unearthly moans rising up as she demolished them. They all lunged and clawed for her, yet, despite their greater size, none stood a chance. Within moments, hundreds lay dead on the bridge, lumps of blackened tar, and with each kill, she felt more powerful than she'd ever had.

Khtha grimaced as he stepped toward her, holding out his palm, clearly frustrated. A red beam of light emitted from it, but Kyra was unafraid. She held out her own palm, sensing her innate power was now stronger than his. White light shot forth, and as it met his beam of light, it made it dissolve.

Khtha stared back, clearly stunned and horrified.

He slowly lowered his palm, as if in defeat, and Kyra felt a tremendous power rush through her palm, a power stronger than she'd ever felt. It was the power she had been born with, the power she had been afraid to embrace until now. It was one that she finally allowed herself to embrace, now, as leader of Escalon. If not on behalf of herself, she could embrace it on behalf of all her people.

She raised her palm higher and intensified the light, and as she did, Khtha finally sank to his knees, crying out. Kyra walked forward, continuing to push the light down toward him. Soon, he slumped over to his side. She could feel his evil power, one that had lasted for thousands of years, that had supported Ra, had supported all of the Pandesian Empire, leaving him.

A huge ball of white light suddenly shot forth from her palm and consumed him. A moment later, Kyra felt a rush of victory as he disappeared, all that remained a pile of robes on the ground.

A hole opened in the earth, a column of black light shot up, and Khtha's shrieks echoed as he was sucked down below ground, the hole sealing up after his departure. Kyra felt a rush of satisfaction knowing that this horrible creature had been extinguished for good.

As Khtha sank below the earth, there came an awful moaning, and Kyra looked out to see the army of black creatures rising from the Fields of Ore suddenly melt back into the earth, disintegrating now that their master was dead. She breathed a sigh of relief, her shoulders aching, still out of breath from the battle.

Yet her relief was tempered by a fresh concern: on the horizon she spotted, marching for the bridge, millions more fresh Pandesian soldiers.

Reinforcements had arrived.

If they reached the bridge, if they crossed into Escalon, everything they fought for would be finished.

Kyra stood on the bridge, breathing hard, and faced off, finally alone against Ra. His army lay in the distance behind him, and hers behind her. Finally, their time had come.

Ra raised his golden sword and grimaced, stepping forward.

"You imagine yourself to be strong now," he spat, "because you killed a few monsters and a sorcerer past his prime. Yet you are nothing. You are but a girl, and will always be nothing. I am everything. You cannot kill the Great and Holy Ra. I have never been killed and I shall never be killed. I am a god—and man cannot defeat a god."

Ra scowled and suddenly charged, slashing down at her with his great sword, groaning as he lowered it for her head. She held her ground, fearless, raising the Staff of Truth, confident in her powers.

Kyra blocked his blow amidst a great clang and shower of sparks, managing to stop his sword in midair. She then stepped forward, filled with the certainty of her own powers, and kicked him in the chest.

She watched as the great Ra went flying back, airborne, thirty feet. He landed hard on his back and went sliding across the bridge.

Ra lay there and looked up, wide-eyed, clearly stunned.

Kyra approached and he stood, wiped blood off his mouth with the back of his hand, and grimaced. He raised his sword and, letting out a fierce battle cry, charged once again.

This time Ra slashed back and forth, again and again, the blade whistling through the air, lunging for her.

Kyra forced herself to remain calm. She sidestepped as one blow smashed into the side of the bridge, strong enough to take out a chunk of it. He slashed again, a blow strong enough to cut three men in half, and again she dodged and the sword took out another chunk of bridge.

Kyra, more focused than she had ever been, finally understood what it meant to be in the moment. Feeling the power of her ancestors course through her, the power passed down to her in her bloodline through her mother, she swung the Staff of Truth in between his blows and smashed him across the jaw.

A cracking noise split the air as the blow sent Ra flying back a good twenty feet, until he smashed against the stone railing of the bridge. He lay there in a heap, unmoving.

Kyra walked over to him, seeing the power slowly ebbing from him, seeing his look of hubris slowly morph to one of uncertainty. It was a magical thing to watch. And it gave her satisfaction. For her people.

For her father.

Indeed, she felt her father's spirit looking down, coursing through her.

Kyra leaned over, grabbed his chest, and pulled him up. He grimaced down at her as she held him up high overhead with one hand, feeling more powerful than ever. She looked deep into his eyes, the soulless black eyes of her foe, of the man she would vanquish.

"For my father," she said calmly.

Kyra threw him, sending him sliding forty feet across the bridge, smashing into the rail on the far side.

Ra crawled to his hands and knees, coughing up blood, then finally stumbled to his feet. He looked unsure as he raised his sword and pathetically charged for her.

"No one can kill the Great and Holy Ra!" he shouted. "NO ONE!"

He charged this time with both hands holding the sword high overhead, aiming for her head, to kill her once and for all. Kyra did not wait. She charged forward with all she had, racing to greet him before he could her. As she ran forward with lightning speed, she let out a great battle cry herself, feeling the power of the world course through her. She raced forward and lunged the Staff of Truth through his chest. The Staff of Truth magically sharpened at its tip, as if anticipating her needs and morphing to suit her. Ra shrieked as it punctured him, and went out the other side.

Ra fell to his knees and dropped his weapon, gushing blood. He looked up at Kyra with eyes wide in shock.

"You…have…killed…what…could…not…be…killed,"   he struggled to say.

And then he dropped face first to the ground.

Dead.

Kyra felt a rush of satisfaction, as she felt her father's spirit shining down on her, avenged. She felt Escalon, avenged. She felt her mother smiling down with pride, felt her destiny fulfilled. The ruler of the vast Pandesian Empire, of most the world, was dead at her hands. She had become the warrior they had always dreamt she would be; she had become the leader of Escalon, cutting off the head of the great Empire.

Yet Kyra had little time to reflect on her victory. A million of his men still marched for the gate, while behind her Anvin and his men fought off what remained of the Pandesian army inside Escalon, and Theon fought for his survival

A rumble like thunder shook the earth, and Kyra spun to see one of the four beasts dive down and smash into the earth right beside Theon, grabbing Theon's tail with its claws and hurling him. Her heart dropped to watch Theon spin end over end through the air. He landed on hard rock, tumbling in a great cloud of dust.

The other three beasts followed, close on Theon's tails. Yet Kyra watched with pride as Theon spun, jumped to his feet, and sank his teeth into one beast's throat as it lunged to finish him off. Theon caught the beast by surprise, unwilling to let go. The beast writhed every which way, trying to shake Theon off, but was unable to. Theon held on for dear life, even as he was smashed into rock on either side, and finally the massive beast stopped writhing, limp.

Dead.

No sooner had it died than the three others pounced on Theon's back. Kyra's heart slammed; she knew that if she didn't do something soon he would die.

Kyra sprinted across the bridge and as she reached the far side, cracked one of the beasts across the back with the Staff of Truth. She felt the vibration of the staff course up and down her arms as a white light shot forth from it, and she heard the crack reverberate. The creature shrieked and spun for her, and as it did, she cracked it across the face.

She felt the definitive power of the blow. It suddenly stiffened and dropped to its side, dead.

Another beast jumped off Theon's back, snarled, and lunged for her, coming at her with lightning speed. The Staff of Truth hummed in her hand, and, listening to it, she raised it and threw it.

The staff buzzed through the air like a spear and pierced the beast's chest, all the way through and out the other side. It landed face-first in the dirt and slid all the way up to Kyra's feet, dead.

The fourth and final beast jumped off of Theon and turned for Kyra, but as it flew for her, Theon rose from the ground, leapt into the air behind it, and dropped onto its back. Theon held on for dear life as the creature let out an awful roar, writhing like mad, trying to throw him off but unable. Theon finally managed to slam it down to the ground, pinning it down, wrestling with it, refusing to let go.

The creature rolled, but Theon rolled with it. The two of them rolled, again and again, until finally they neared the edge of the cliff, the roaring waters far below where the Sea of Sorrow met the Sea of Tears. As they rolled one final time, Theon reached up with his talons and dug them into the beast's throat.

The beast shrieked, blood gushing down its scales, and Theon raised it by its throat and threw it.

The creature plummeted through the air, flailing, until it impacted with the sharp rocks below and splashed into the waters, dead. The waters turned red with its blood, and within moments it was swarmed by red sharks.

Kyra breathed deep with relief. She had never been so proud of Theon. She knew that his father, Theos, was looking down with pride, too, at his son. Theon, after all, was the last dragon standing. He had become, as the prophecies had predicted, the King of the Dragons.

Kyra summoned her staff and it came flying through the air and landed in her palm. She turned and looked back out at Anvin and the men, battling what remained of Ra's army, still outnumbering her father's men greatly, with their thousands of soldiers who remained inside of Escalon. Kyra knew she had to help them.

Kyra took off at a sprint. She raised the staff and slashed down through the air as she ran, and it hit the ground with a great cracking noise. A rippling reverberated through the ground as white light emanated from the staff and spread through the Pandesian camp. Kyra watched as several hundred soldiers fell, their cries rising up through the air, the white light destroying them.

The remaining Pandesian soldiers began to turn in panic and run, and Kyra watched with satisfaction as Anvin and his men hunted them down, the momentum finally in their favor. She knew that Anvin and her father's men would fight brilliantly, and that soon enough not a single Pandesian soldier would remain alive on the mainland of Escalon.

Suddenly, though, a rumbling filled the air, and Kyra gripped the staff tight. She felt it humming in her hands as she turned and faced the bridge. She watched as there, on the far side, an entire nation of Pandesian soldiers, reinforcements, crossed the Fields of Ore. It was an unstoppable force, filling the world, and it marched for the Bridge of Sorrows bridge like a nation of ants.

They had already reached it, and as they mounted the bridge, Kyra could feel the ground shaking beneath her. It was like the weight of the world, thunderous, monotonous. She knew that if they reached her side, Escalon would be finished.

Kyra ran to the center of the bridge, knowing she had to be the lure. She had to let as many of them mount the bridge as she could, had to sacrifice herself, if that's what it took, to save Escalon.

Kyra waited and waited, until the soldiers, marching like a drumbeat, filled the bridge, nearly reaching her. They drew their swords in perfect discipline as their commander shouted, and as a horn sounded, the thousands of men came charging right for her.

Kyra waited and waited.

Patience, she urged herself. *Discipline. For your father.*

Finally, as the soldiers were but feet away, Kyra raised the Staff of Truth high and brought it straight down, to the floor of the bridge beneath her feet.

There came a sharp cracking noise as she felt the tremendous power of the staff reverberate through her arm, up through her skull. She felt the bridge of Sorrows, which had lasted for centuries, which had connected Escalon to the mainland for thousands of years, buckle.

A moment later, the bridge split in two and collapsed.

Kyra felt the ground give way, and felt herself plummeting through the air, in free-fall. She knew she was falling to her death.

Yet she felt no fear. After all, the air was filled with Pandesian soldiers, thousands of them, falling all around her. She would, after all, die with honor. It was a noble death, the final piece of the puzzle to free Escalon forever, and it had been worth it.

As Kyra prepared to meet her death, the sea rushing up to meet her, a screech suddenly filled the air. A moment later she felt talons grab her from behind, felt herself being hoisted back up through the air. A moment before she had impacted, she had been saved.

Kyra looked up to see her old friend Theon. He had caught her.

As she flew, she saw millions of Pandesian soldiers trapped on the far side of the ocean, backed up in the Fields of Ore, unable to cross. Escalon, finally, was unreachable.

It was free.

The dream her father, her ancestors, had harbored for thousands of years had come to pass. They were no longer a nation of subjects. They were a nation now of free men and women.

Theon slowly let Kyra down amidst all of her father's men, all shouting triumphantly as they finished off the last of the Pandesians on the mainland. They all turned to her, as one, and let out a great shout. Their cries filled the air as they all looked to her with adulation, as a warrior among men, as their ruler. She felt her father smiling down upon them all.

"Kyra!" they chanted. "Kyra! Kyra!"

EPILOGUE

One sun cycle later

Kyra knelt alone in the dim, cool temple, knees pressing on the freshly hewn marble, feeling the solemn energy around her as she prayed before the newly built altar. She closed her eyes and, as she had for hours, slipped into a deep state of peace and reflection. Outside came muffled shouts of joy, all the people of Escalon, tens of thousands of them, citizens and warriors alike, free men and women and children, congregating upon the new capital. This was a special day. They had come from all corners of the land to celebrate the completion of Escalon's new capital—and to celebrate, more importantly, her wedding day.

Kyra took a deep breath, feeling the enormity of the day before her. Here she was, in the new capital, and she could scarcely believe, after a year of arduous work, it had been completed. She had chosen this place, atop the ruins of the Lost Temple, a sacred spot of ancient spiritual power, where the ancient capital of Escalon had once lain, and under her watchful eye, thousands of Escalonites had labored for one year, quarrying marble from ancient cliffs and erecting this spectacular city by the sea. It was more magnificent than it had ever been, and it would, she knew, serve as a beacon for a new age, a new time. A time of freedom. A time unlike any Escalon had ever known.

The muted cheers of her people brought her back, and Kyra heart lifted her head and smiled to hear them so joyous, more joyous than she had ever remembered her people being. They should be, she realized. After all, Escalon was finally free. Free from the armies of Pandesia, free from the nation of trolls, free from the flocks of dragons. It was the first time in their history that her people could enjoy the land and rest at ease. It was the first time in their history they could usher in a new era of abundance.

Kyra smiled broadly as she thought of Kyle out there, somewhere, getting ready as she was, preparing for their holy matrimony. It felt like a dream. After all the battles, after each coming so close to death, finally, they would be together. It was what her people needed—a new Queen, a new King, a royal couple to preside over the rebuilding and bounty of the land. It was what she needed, too.

Her people had even more reasons to celebrate this day, too: Dierdre and Marco, and Merk and Lorna, had decided to join them in being wed on this auspicious day. It would be a triple wedding for the nation to enjoy, followed by a week of festivities, of dances, feasting, and drinking. Already she could hear the horns sounding, signaling that Motley and his new troupe of actors were starting their performance in their newly built theater. She heard the laughter, and she knew it had begun.

Kyra would join them soon enough. She was still relishing the quiet, the peace in here; she needed time for herself, time to reflect on this holy day. For this day was not only the one-year anniversary of the end of the Great War, of the rise of the dragons, but also the anniversary of her father's death.

Deep inside, commingled with her joy, was a lingering sadness, one she knew would always be with her. He was her father, after all, the man she had loved her entire life. His passing was a deep scar from which she sensed she would never fully recover.

Tainting her joy was also a longing for her mother, especially on this, her wedding day. She lowered her head and clasped her hands, hoping still for a reply.

Mother, where are you?

Kyra had been trying to talk to her mother for a year, ever since she had become leader of this great nation—and to her surprise, she had been met with silence. She kept expecting her mother to appear, to embrace her, to tell her the secret of her identity—anything.

And yet there had been nothing. And that silence gnawed away at Kyra's soul.

Kyra furrowed her brows as she knelt, needing to hear from her mother. Even just one word.

Mother, I need you now.

Kyra became lost in a deep meditation, and after much time passed, she began to sense something. She opened her eyes and blinked. Her heart beat faster.

There, in the darkness, the face of her mother was appearing.

"Mother?" Kyra called out, too excited to get her hopes high.

After a long time, she heard a voice.

"It is I, Kyra," the voice replied. "You have summoned me. And I am more proud of you on this day than I can ever say."

Kyra felt tears of sadness, mixed with joy, run down her face.

"I miss my father," she said, surprised to find herself crying. "Very much."

Her mother smiled back, reassuring.

"He is here with me now," she replied. "He loves you and is looking down on you."

Kyra felt her tears flow as she tried to steady herself inside

"What is it you seek, Kyra?" her mother asked.

Kyra reflected, trying to know what it was that she so desperately needed to hear from her mother.

"I need answers, Mother. You never told me. I seek to know who I am. Who *you* are."

A long silence followed. Her mother looked back at her for a long time, her eyes shining blue. And finally, she nodded back and took a deep breath.

"I am of the ancient ones," she replied. "Many millennia ago a prophecy was read to me, of the daughter I would have. The one who would change the fate of Escalon. The one who would rule the world one day. The one who is partly of us, yet partly human. The one true warrior."

Her mother paused.

"That is you, Kyra. You are the chosen one. You are the leader, the warrior, that Escalon has always needed. You cannot even imagine the greatness that lies before you. You cannot even imagine the life you are going to lead, the worlds you are going to conquer. All of this, all that has happened, is but a prologue of your life to come."

Kyra marveled, wondering what other twists and turns her life could possibly hold in store, what could possibly be bigger, more dramatic, than all that had already happened.

"I did not choose your father from amongst my people," her mother continued, "but from the human race. I did not choose him from a line of kings. I searched far and wide for the man with the bravest heart, the strongest soul. Your lineage is your honor, your courage, your valor—more precious than any gems or royal bloodline."

She paused.

"Too many people knew of the prophecy," she continued. "Ancient Ones, rival kings, dark forces, all wanting you dead. The nation of dragons, too, wanted to seek you out, to tear you apart. You had to be hidden, Kyra. Your identity had to be kept secret, even from yourself."

She paused, and Kyra's mind reeled as she took it all in.

"You are your mother's daughter," she continued. "And you are your father's daughter, too. Most of all, you are yourself. A human with powers, powers that are imperfect, yet still more perfect than any human's. They are powers you can access if you believe in yourself—and powers that will fail you if you do not. They are powers built on faith. And faith, after all, Kyra, is all that we have.

"You are a very special hybrid, Kyra. There has never been anyone like you, and there never will be again. You have saved this land. You have made us all proud. Trust in yourself. Believe in your powers, and you shall rule Escalon forever. Yet remember: you also have the same power to fall into darkness. Use your powers wisely, and always stay in the light."

Kyra's heart pounded in her chest as she listened, all of it, her entire life, finally falling into place, finally making sense. She sensed it all to be true, and she felt closer to her mother than ever. She felt a great tension leaving her body as the truth was finally revealed.

And then, suddenly, her mother approached, walking out of the mist. Kyra's breath froze in her throat. There was her mother, no longer a vision, but a real woman standing before her, stepping forward to embrace Kyra.

Kyra rose and threw her arms over her mother, embracing her with all she had. She wept as she felt her real mother in her arms for the first time, finally, for the first time, feeling at home in the world.

"I love you, Kyra," her mother whispered into her ear. "I always have, and I always will."

"I love *you*, Mother."

And just as she finished uttering the words, suddenly, her mother was gone.

Kyra, now holding air, turned every which way, perplexed. She searched all the dark corners of the temple, yet saw nothing but the soft incense that hung in the air. Had it all been an illusion?

No. Kyra was certain it had not. Indeed, she looked down at her finger, feeling something, and she saw a glistening ring, one that had not been there before. It was purple, lined with sapphires. She knew her mother had placed it there. She closed her hand and opened it, marveling at the sparkling jewel, feeling the power of it. Feeling her mother now with her forever.

Kyra took a deep breath and slowly released it. She felt a great sense of peace. She felt her soul was restored.

She was ready, now, to face the world.

*

Aidan stood amidst the thick crowd in the grand, newly erected amphitheatre, swaying every which way as thousands of Escalonites gathered in close, all crowding the stage to watch Motley and his troupe give their wedding day performance. Cassandra by his side, White at his feet, contentedly eating scraps of meat off the floor,

Aidan looked up and watched with pride as Motley gave the performance of a lifetime, keeping the entire crowd laughing with their comedy.

"I say, my dear wife, what are we having for dinner tonight?" Motley asked the actor on stage beside him.

"Whatever you decide to make me," replied the actress.

The crowd broke into laughter as the farcical comedy went on and on. Aidan was glued by Motley's wide array of comical expressions, and he could not help laughing himself. Motley had a special comic talent, strong enough to keep this entire city mesmerized, and he was on fine display today.

Aidan surveyed the stage and marveled that his acting troupe was now ten times the size it had been when they'd first met; he was even more in awe at the new amphitheatre, massive, holding tens of thousands of people, and he was filled with pride knowing that Kyra had assured it was built for them as the centerpiece of the new capital. She had put fantasy first, had given the actors the glory that had never been afforded to them in Escalon before. Motley thrived, seeming like a new man.

He deserved it, Aidan thought. He was, after all, no mere actor, but also a hero of the Great War. Finally, he and his actors could be respected in this land as much as warriors. In this new Escalon, under his sister's direction, there was equal glory, side by side, for both war and art.

Aidan felt a squeeze of his hand and he looked over to see Cassandra smiling. Shaken from his reverie, he smiled back at her.

"Shall we leave this place?" she asked. "I would rather talk to you than hear this play again."

Aidan nodded and led her out of the crowd, pushing their way through the mob, White joining them and snatching a piece of chicken out of an unsuspecting person's hand, until finally they all exited the soaring, arched stone gates of the theater.

The crowds gone, the noise behind them, finally they could breathe again. Aidan took a deep breath and led her as they strolled through the new, shining white marble streets of the capital, White running excitedly up ahead of them, smelling everything.

Aidan took it all in as they went, as in awe as he was the first time he had seen it. Not only was the city new, but everything on this day was strewn with roses and elaborate wreaths, the red flower petals complementing the shining white marble. Warm summer winds rolled in off the ocean, ripe fruit and flowers hung from bushes and trees all around them, and it felt like no Escalon he had ever known. This coast was so different from the cold, howling winds of the northwest, of Volis, and he admired Kyra's foresight and wisdom in choosing to build the new capital here. Their ancestors had had it right, and she had wisely deferred to their wisdom.

The new capital, built high up on the cliffs, towered over the sea, and the sparkling blue of the ocean reflected into the city and bounced off of everything. The ancient ruins of the Lost Temple had been preserved, though, and gracefully incorporated into the new capital, adding a sense of history. As he and Cassandra walked down wide, gorgeous boulevards framed by trees and neat rows of grass, he passed soaring, ancient columns, fragments of temples and buildings, the living history of their forefathers everywhere in this place. It gave him a sense of continuity he had never felt in the old capital.

The two of them walked in a comfortable silence for a long time, enjoying each other's company, neither feeling the need to speak. After all, they had been through so much together, they could nearly read each other's thoughts.

"My sister weds today," he finally said to her, breaking the silence.

She nodded back and smiled.

"I know," she replied. "The entire capital knows. Not only your sister, but Dierdre and Marco, and Lorna and Merk shall wed, too."

Aidan walked aimlessly, and realized he was leading them to a place he had not expected to go. They turned down a street and he looked up to see before him the wide circular plaza in the center of the city, dominated by a huge monument in its center. He stood before the immense, shining statue of his father.

At the base of the statue was a bubbling fountain, surrounded by fresh flowers, and before this was an ever-burning flame, its flames rippling in a huge, black granite bowl. Aidan felt a wave of sadness as he stepped forward and looked down at them. He could not bring himself on this day to look up at the visage of his father, as he usually did. Instead, he struggled to suppress his tears as he remembered the war, his father's death, his brothers' death, the death of so many warriors he'd loved.

White, at Aidan's side, whined, and Aidan reached down and stroked his head.

"Your father loved you very much," Cassandra said. "I could see it in his eyes. He was so proud of you. I know he's looking down on you now."

Aidan smiled, filled with sadness.

"Our time was cut short," Aidan said. "I never had time to show him the man I could be."

Cassandra squeezed his hand.

"Maybe all you were was enough. Have you ever considered that?"

Aidan pondered her words as he took a deep breath and wiped away a tear. He finally turned and squeezed Cassandra's hand and looked into her eyes. He reached into his pocket, hands trembling as he began to do something he realized he'd been wanting to do for a long time.

"Before my father died," Aidan said, "he gave me this ring. It was his mother's, and her mother's before her. He told me that when I found the girl I love, to give it to her."

Cassandra looked down, eyes wide with surprise, as he placed it on her finger.

"I hope you shall accept it as a promise ring," he said. "When we are older, one day, I wish to wed you and no one else."

Cassandra looked up at him and her eyes welled with tears.

She leaned in and kissed him.

"I would like that," she said. "I would like that very much."

*

Kyra, accompanied by a dozen royal bridesmaids, walked slowly down the wide boulevard, making her way toward the towering altar. Throngs squeezed her in on all sides, showering her with rose petals, and she felt the solemn joy to the air. She wore a magnificent wedding dress, hand-sewn by Escalon tailors who had worked on it for moons, its long train trailing behind her. Holding it was Dierdre, who had become a fast friend, one of the few friends she had left from the Great War. It served a double purpose, as Dierdre was walking down the aisle herself to a waiting Marco. Lorna held it, too, on her other side, as she walked down to a waiting Merk.

As they walked, they passed between ancient soaring columns and beneath the magnificent arches that had been preserved from the days of the Lost Temple. She passed by the old and the new, all commingled in this new capital, the new armory to one side, where all the new knights, in their shiniest armor, came forth to march toward the wedding ceremony. She passed the new Hall of Heroes on her other side, passed the abundant statues and monuments to the Great War, passed the grand new Feasting Hall, the barracks for her new royal guard. She passed a marble statue of Alec, kneeling, thrusting the Unfinished Sword into the Tower of Ur, and Dierdre paused to place a fresh flower in its well.

A solemn tune filled the air, played by royal musicians flanking the aisle, a mix of lutes and flutes and harps. As Kyra listened, it brought back memories, of growing up in Volis with her father and brothers, of when life had been so simple, so filled with hope for the future. She wondered how one person could live so many lives in one lifetime, how one year could give way to such a radically different year, how time could always march on so relentlessly. The tune stirred her soul, honored the dead, and toward its climax, became more hopeful, offering a vision of a new future.

Kyra looked out and saw the massive altar looming before her, a hundred feet high, framed by ancient columns, and at its center, smiling, waiting for them all, Kyle. He was flanked by Marco and Merk, waiting for their brides, too, and they were joined by Anvin, Seavig, Kavos, Bramthos and a dozen of her father's men, all in full suits of shining armor. Kyra glanced over and saw Aidan and Cassandra seated in the front row, smiling back, Motley beside them, White and Leo at their feet. Off to the side, she saw Andor, snorting contentedly, bedecked in a white shawl for the day.

Kyle stared down at her, and Kyra fell in love all over again. He had sacrificed everything for her, so many times. His love had sustained her through the worst of times, had kept her alive through the Great War, through her father's death, and beyond. Now, as she ruled Escalon, he would be at her side.

As Kyra finally reached the altar, thousands of eyes upon her, Kyle stepped down and took her hand. As he did, the crowd gasped in delight. Marco and Merk stepped down and took Dierdre's and Lorna's hands, too.

As Kyra stepped up to the altar, Anvin, who had been like an uncle to her, smiled reassuringly.

"Your father is looking down," he said, "and he is proud."

Seeing Anvin reminded her of her father, and Kyra had to restrain herself to not tear up. Beside him stood her real uncle, Kolva, who stepped forward and laid a comforting hand on her elbow, guiding her the last honorary step.

Standing in the center, presiding over the ceremony, was Alva. Smaller than them all, he wore a shining white robe, and yet his presence loomed larger than all of them.

Alva slammed his staff down on the marble three times, slowly, and the thousands of knights and citizens of Escalon all slowly quieted and took their seats. He raised his staff high in the air, and Kyra could feel the power emanating off of it.

Not a sound could be heard but for the soft, distant crashing of the ocean waves and the whistling of the gales of wind off the ocean, sweeping over the capital.

"Kyra, Queen of Escalon," Alva began, his voice rolling off the ancient walls, "the one and only great ruler of our people, it is my great honor to wed you today in matrimony to Kyle of the Watchers, another selfless hero of our people and our time."

Kyra felt Kyle squeeze her hand, while Alva turned to the others.

"Dierdre, you shall be wed to Marco, and Lorna, you shall be wed to Merk. These three couples have chosen to wed on the same day, and this shall serve as a sign of a new Escalon, a foundation for the new generation to come."

Alva turned to the masses.

"Today is the day we put all evils behind us. For as sure as night gives way to day, evil gives way to joy, violence to victory, and darkness to light, times of sorrow become times of joy, times of scarcity, prosperity, and times of danger, safety. And this a day of all days, a day when the dials turn from darkness to joy."

The crowd cheered softly, and Alva took a deep breath.

"Life is a great cycle," he finally continued. "And as the world turns one way today, it will turn another tomorrow. The same will be true of your marriage. Remember to always be true to yourself, and to uphold the great virtues of Escalon. Honor, valor, loyalty— these will sustain you through all turnings of the wheel of time, and of destiny. Remember: the wheel will always turn, but its center remains the same. If you choose to live in the center of the wheel, steadfast and sturdy to who you are, to your virtues, its spokes will never turn you."

Kyra pondered his words, overwhelmed by his intensity, feeling the spirit of her mother and father shining down upon her. A deep and long silence filled the air, and Kyra felt frozen in time.

Finally, Alva spoke again.

"Kyra, do you take Kyle to be your husband, and Kyle, do you take Kyra to be your wife, for now and forever, to serve and protect each other, to defend your nation of Escalon?"

They turned to each other, and each smiled.

"I do," they each said at once.

Kyle, eyes aglow, leaned in, as Kyra did, and they both kissed. The crowds cheered.

Alva asked the same of Lorna and Merk, and of Dierdre and Marco, and as they answered in the affirmative and kissed their new spouse, the crowd cheered again.

Kyra felt lost in that kiss, felt as if she were born anew. She felt a new age, a new dawn, a new life spreading through her. She felt that she could live again. That she was being given *permission* to live again.

There came a great shout of joy, of triumph, and she and Kyle were suddenly covered in a shower of flowers, as all of Escalon, overjoyed, celebrating, erupted in a great cheer. There came a roar, and Kyra looked up, with the rest of the masses, and was thrilled to see Theon, circling overhead, diving down low, then swooping up again, his loving presence felt amongst them all. As he dove up he breathed a long streak of fire, and the crowd gasped in delight as it filled the skies to mark the occasion.

Kyra had never felt as happy as she did in this moment. She embraced Kyle and looked up at the sky, and she could have sworn in that moment that she saw her mother's and father's faces shining down on her. They were each so proud, so filled with love. And in that sky a new light seemed to shine. It was a new light spreading over Escalon. She knew in that moment that life could flourish again, that a new generation could rise up out of the ashes, one that did not know of the sorrows of the past. Maybe one day she could even have a child of her own. A child who knew nothing but peace, prosperity, joy, freedom.

Despite everything that had happened, all the tragedy they had endured, life refused to give up, she realized. Love was stronger even than death, could triumph over death. *If* she allowed it to. It was the coward's way to fold, she realized. Only heroes were brave enough to live on through tragedy.

Despite all the death, all the sorrow, could she be brave enough to live again? That was the question she pondered as she held Kyle tight.

And finally, as Kyra took a deep breath, she realized the answer.

Yes. She could.

Author Note

I am honored that you've finished this series, and am so grateful to all of you for reading.

One day I may revisit Kyra and her dramatic future in Escalon, in a separate series.

But for now, I am thrilled to announce that I am working hard on a new fantasy series, OF CROWNS AND GLORY. The first book, SLAVE, WARRIOR, QUEEN will publish this April. I would be so honored if you continue on this journey with me.

COMING IN APRIL, 2016

SLAVE, WARRIOR, QUEEN
(Of Crowns and Glory—Book 1)

17 year old Adina, a beautiful, poor girl in the Empire city of Ceres, lives the harsh and unforgiving life of a commoner. By day she delivers her father's forged weapons to the palace training grounds, and by night she secretly trains with them, yearning to be a warrior in a land where girls are forbidden to fight. With her pending sale to slavehood, she is desperate.

18 year old Prince Thanos despises everything his royal family stands for. He abhors their harsh treatment of the masses, especially the brutal competition—The Killings—that lies at the heart of the city. He yearns to break free from the restraints of his upbringing, yet he, a fine warrior, sees no way out.

When Adina stuns the court with her hidden powers, she finds herself wrongfully imprisoned, doomed to an even worse life than she could imagine. Thanos, smitten, must choose if he will risk it all for her. Yet, thrust into a world of duplicity and deadly secrets, Adina quickly learns there are those who rule, and those who are their pawns. And that sometimes, being chosen is the worst that can happen.

SLAVE, WARRIOR, QUEEN tells an epic tale of tragic love, vengeance, betrayal, ambition, and destiny. Filled with unforgettable characters and heart-pounding action, it transports us into a world we will never forget, and makes us fall in love with fantasy all over again.

Books by Morgan Rice

OF CROWNS AND GLORY
SLAVE, WARRIOR, QUEEN (BOOK #1)

KINGS AND SORCERERS
RISE OF THE DRAGONS
RISE OF THE VALIANT
THE WEIGHT OF HONOR
A FORGE OF VALOR
A REALM OF SHADOWS
NIGHT OF THE BOLD

THE SORCERER'S RING
A QUEST OF HEROES
A MARCH OF KINGS
A FATE OF DRAGONS
A CRY OF HONOR
A VOW OF GLORY
A CHARGE OF VALOR
A RITE OF SWORDS
A GRANT OF ARMS
A SKY OF SPELLS
A SEA OF SHIELDS
A REIGN OF STEEL
A LAND OF FIRE
A RULE OF QUEENS
AN OATH OF BROTHERS
A DREAM OF MORTALS

THE SURVIVAL TRILOGY
ARENA ONE (Book #1)
ARENA TWO (Book #2)

the Vampire Journals
turned (book #1)
loved (book #2)
betrayed (book #3)
destined (book #4)
desired (book #5)
betrothed (book #6)
vowed (book #7)
found (book #8)
resurrected (book #9)
craved (book #10)
fated (book #11)
obsessed (book #12)

About Morgan Rice

Morgan Rice is the #1 bestselling and USA Today bestselling author of the epic fantasy series THE SORCERER'S RING, comprising seventeen books; of the #1 bestselling series THE VAMPIRE JOURNALS, comprising eleven books (and counting); of the #1 bestselling series THE SURVIVAL TRILOGY, a post-apocalyptic thriller comprising two books (and counting); and of the new epic fantasy series KINGS AND SORCERERS. Morgan's books are available in audio and print editions, and translations are available in over 25 languages.

Morgan's new epic fantasy series, OF CROWNS AND GLORY, will publish in April, 2016, beginning with book #1, SLAVE, WARRIOR, QUEEN.

Morgan loves to hear from you, so please feel free to visit www.morganricebooks.com to join the email list, receive a free book, receive free giveaways, download the free app, get the latest exclusive news, connect on Facebook and Twitter, and stay in touch!

Made in the USA
Lexington, KY
05 October 2017